Infatuated

Razor

Ahsyad Publication

www.ahsyadpublication.com

Infatuated

ISBN 13:978-0615997841

ISBN 10:0615997848

Ahsyad Publication is dedicated to producing
innovative stories, told from a fresh perspec-
tive, with memorable characters. This is a work
of Fiction. Names, places, incidents and characters are products of the authors imagination
and used fictitiously. Any resemblances to an
actual person living or deceased are entirely
coincidental.

Acknowledgements:

Where do I start? Man this has been a long journey that I never thought would happen. First, of course, I thank God. You brought me through some hard times and I'm still standing due to you. I would like to thank: Dee Dee M. Scott for this major opportunity. You believed in my work and got me; the person and the writer. Thank you for giving my baby a home! To the entire Ahsyad Publication Team: Monica Wilson, you are one hell of a publicist! You got this country boy coverage and treated me like a star. To Tara Washington. You stayed on me and motivated me to finish this assignment. Brooklyn Darkchild, I love the way you edited my book. You understood my writing style and got me. Last but not least: to my Family in Marion, S.C, The Andersons': Ruth, Bobby,

Johnny, Lil' Mo, Shawn and Ruby; My kids! We did it! I love ya'll to death! And anyone I forgot it was my head; not my heart so I say it now: Thank ya'll!!!

Razor

Please join our mailing list on FaceBook at:

Ahsyad Publication Bookreaders to stay updated on upcoming books!

Prologue

Kendra

My eyes open slowly. I want to scream but I can't speak. Rainbow-colored lights flash overhead. Chaos moves all around me: people picking at my body, sticking me in my arm, and someone even puts some kind of tubing around my head, adjusting it under my nose. I try to lift my arms to snatch the tube off, but my arms feel like dead weight. I look at the overhead lights again. All I can think about is my husband, Rich. Damn, I love him. We've been married for five years, and I still get chills when I see him. Rich is cute as hell: six foot one, built like a football player, light brown skin, bow-legs, and the biggest hazel eyes I've ever seen. We would have been perfect together, only—

"SHE'S GOING INTO SHOCK!" a woman dressed in all white shouts.

She and another man lift me from a stretcher and place me on what feels like a hard table.

Shock? What the hell is that? All I know is I'm tired. More tired than I've ever been in my life. I can't take in even one lungful of air and I don't feel anything. My eyes feel like they're turning into hard marbles.

Another man dressed in all white hovers over me.

"LET'S GET HER TO THE OPERATING ROOM, NOW!" he shouts.

I want to ask him what's going on. Why is he shouting in my ear? And where is my daughter, Bree? Worried out of my mind, I try to sit up, but it feels like a sumo wrestler is on my chest. Everything starts moving in slow motion, then the world slowly begins to fade away.

About ten people push my bed down a long corridor. It feels like I'm being sucked down a drain. Lifting my head a little, I look at the wet red shirt I'm wearing. My memory comes rushing back. The shirt isn't red—my upper body is covered with blood from the gunshot wound my husband inflicted on me.

My mind flashes back to a few months earlier, and the day my descent to Hell began…

1

Kendra

Rich ain't never done nothing but work and sleep. Sometimes we'd make love, but he didn't even want to halfway do that right. I didn't want to have sex all the time, but when I wanted it, I wanted it done right—my way. Rich hated when I took control. He wouldn't let me get on top and he knew that was my favorite position. He wanted to do the same tired position—all the time: climb on top of me then pound away for five minutes—no foreplay, no nothing. Then he'd collapse and ask for the remote or another slice of whatever desert I'd made that day with dinner. By the time I brought desert back he'd be snoring, and I'd be horny and lonely with nothing but the LMN Movie Channel to keep me company for the rest of the night. My friend, April, told me not to be so hard on Rich. She said no marriage was perfect and things would get better. April had no clue how thin my patience was running with Rich. Sometimes I just wanted to walk out my front door and never look back. If it wasn't for our daughter, Bree, I probably would have already done it.

I thought Rich had his priorities ass backwards. He loved his job at CC Electric more than me and his daughter. He loved it so much he talked about it in his sleep. He even talked about it over breakfast—dinner, too. In fact, the only real conversations we had were about his job. I didn't have to worry about him messing with another woman because all of his time was divided between the four things he loved the most: work, sleep, his friend Cory and video games. And poor old me, I got the measly minutes in between.

The way I saw it, I didn't get married to be lonely, and I damned sure didn't get married to be ignored—which is what Rich did most of the time. Treated me like I was invisible. Pulling compliments from him was like trying to pull out a wisdom tooth with my bare hands. I could be dressed in my best outfit or butt naked and he'd looked at me the same way. He got more excited over a television show or a new video game. The only compliment I would get was: 'You look alright.' Really? Just Alright? After I'd spent hours fixing my multicolored tresses. Did he realize I was a woman? I wanted to be complimented, adored, pampered and desired. Not taken for granted. I wanted to be wined and dined and live a fantasy sometimes. Waking up to the same thing day in and day out was becoming depressing and redundant.

"Well, I'm not gonna be alone today," I mumbled.

Fed up, I walked into the airy family room, where Rich had been since he got off work this morning at five.

"Rich, wake up!" I nagged. As usual, he was snoozing on his lazy boy with a dirty dish on the table next to him that he must have fixed when he came in from work. Rich was clad in boxers and socks; his work clothes were all over the floor instead of in the hamper in the next room.

"What you want?" Sounding groggy, Rich opened his eyes part way. He ran his hand over his crinkly, short cut hair and turned his buff frame slightly on the recliner, falling back asleep.

"I said get up!" I snatched the pillow from underneath his head.

"What's wrong?" he snapped, sitting up and looking sleepy. "Is something wrong with Bree?"

"No, nothing's wrong with Bree. She's asleep," I said. "I just wanted to see if we could go out today. This is the last weekend before school starts and I haven't been anyplace the entire summer."

"You woke me up for that?" Rich yawned and then gave me a indifferent wave before relaxing again. "Why don't you call up your friend April and go out with her."

"Are you gonna keep Bree?"

"Take her with you," Rich mumbled, yawning again and wiping slob from the corner of his mouth.

"I need a break," I shouted. "Come on."

I shoved him.

"I need a break, too," Rich said, closing his eyes. "I'm the one who's been working six days a week."

I threw the pillow at him, and he had the nerve to grab it, tuck it under his head, and fall back asleep.

For the entire five years we'd been married I'd been begging him to spend time with me. I wish I could say there was a time when Rich was attentive: took me out to parks, picnics, bought me roses—that type of stuff, but Rich had always been Rich—a workaholic. I think I fell in love with him for one: because of his looks, and two: I was young. We got married when I was nineteen and Rich was twenty. Now twenty-four, I felt like I was wasting my time and my life trying to change this man. I wondered what I'd have to do to get his attention—to get him to realize I was a woman with needs. I wasn't dead yet but he made me feel that way, taking me for granted and treating me like a thing instead of a person. I didn't know how much more I could stand. There was no reason for me to be locked up in the house on a beautiful day like this. No reason at all.

"Are you gonna sleep all day?" I shoved him again.

Rich let out a snort and opened his eyes.

"It's two o'clock in the afternoon," I fumed as I marched to the shades. It didn't help that our next door neighbor was outside with her husband

and two kids stuffing suitcases into their car, dressed like they were headed for the beach. I loved the beaches in South Carolina, and the fact that I couldn't go really pissed me off. I left the shades open, drowning Rich in sunlight.

"Come on Kendra," Rich complained. "Let me sleep."

"You've slept long enough. Get your ass up!"

"I'm tired. I'll take you and Bree out tomorrow on my day off. I promise."

Before his head hit the pillow, he was snoring again.

Feeling depressed, I shook my head and dropped to the loveseat in front of Rich. The house was dead. I couldn't wait for school to start Monday so I could return to work at Creekside Elementary where I was a Teacher's Assistant. Man, things really are bad when I dream about going back to work. But at least I'd get out of the house for a few hours and not have to be pressed down taking care of Bree or my daddy twenty-four hours a day.

I decided to finish the housework. In the kitchen, I opened the dishwasher and loaded the plates, forks and knives. Just when I was about to load the cups, the doorbell chimed. I knew it wasn't nobody for me. The only friend I had who visited was April, and she was busy moving into her new house this weekend. Maybe it was Rich's friend Cory, or someone for my dad.

When I pulled the door open I was smacked dead in the face by a massive tower of chocolate muscles, looming over six feet tall. My heart jumped into my throat. All I could see were parts of him: the coffee-brown skin, smooth-shaven head, ink black eyebrows, long lashes, sterling gray eyes, dimples, plump lips, bulging biceps, and teeth so white and straight he could have been on a dental commercial. I felt like I was going into cardiac arrest. Who was this man, looking like he'd just stepped off the cover of a Men's Fitness magazine?

"May I speak to Kendra?" he asked in a heavily accented voice.

He extended his hand. I shook my head, trying to clear it.

"And you are?" I asked, returning the handshake.

"Kwame. Your friend April said you needed a landscaper to take care of your yard."

"Oh, yeah," I said, trying to slow my breathing.

Kwame's gaze scanned my 34C chest, slim waist, and long legs encased in a pair of skinny jeans.

"May I come in?"

"Yes," I said, stepping aside and inviting him into the two-story brick house. I watched Kwame walk past me, smelling just as good as he looked. Tight ass, muscles flexing.

My God, he was making some woman some-where very happy, I thought. I left the door open, allowing the slight summer breeze to cool me down.

"You have a beautiful home," Kwame complimented the large southern layout.

"Thank you," I responded, quickly locking the screen door.

"And this must be your daughter," Kwame guessed.

I turned to find my four-year-old daughter Bree standing in the middle of the floor, drooling and staring into space.

"Yes."

"What's your name, little one?" Kwame squatted in front of her and pulled a lollypop from the small bag he was carrying. Bree just stood there looking past him with a cloudy look in her eyes. I rushed to her and took the lollypop from him.

"Her name is Bree," I said quickly. "She doesn't talk."

"Oh, she's a shy one," he said, stroking her chubby cheeks.

"No." I answered, wrapping my arms around Bree's shoulders. "She has Autism."

Kwame looked unfazed by what I'd just told him.

"She looks just like you," he said as he stood, towering over me. "Very beautiful."

My heart did a cartwheel. I needed to sit down before my legs gave out. Offering him a seat on the deluxe recliner, I sat Bree at her finger fun table before taking a seat across from him.

"Do you own this house?" Kwame asked, glancing around again.

"My daddy owns it," I answered, playing with Bree's long pigtails nervously. "He's older and sick. I'm talking care of it for him."

"So, I'll be handling business through you, correct?" He focused his gray eyes on me and grinned just enough for me to see his deep dimples. I tried not to stare, but the man was beautiful.

"Yeah," I stuttered, "me or my husband, Rich."

I could have sworn I saw a look of disappointment wash over his striking face, but he recovered too quickly for me to confirm it.

Clearing his throat, Kwame opened a notebook.

"Well, I looked over your yard and I have a lot of ideas. I'd like to add rosebushes, and rocks for the driveway…"

"I love roses. They are my favorite. And rocks for the driveway sound great. But for now, I only need you to cut my grass and trim the hedges once a week. How much would something like that cost?"

"You have a very big yard," Kwame paused as if deep in thought. "Ninety dollars is the cheapest I could go."

"Ninety dollars," I repeated. That wasn't too steep considering our yard sat on a two-acre plot. I knew I wouldn't find anybody else in their right mind who would cut it for cheaper in this one-hundred-plus degree weather.

"I would be willing to drop the price to fifty, under one condition."

Kwame's eyes narrowed then zoomed in on me. My clitoris began throbbing. I dropped my gaze to Bree so he wouldn't see the effect he was having on me.

"And what is that condition?" I probed coyly.

"It's scorching hot outside. Supply me with plenty of iced water," he smiled devilishly, showing those double dimples.

~~~~

I laughed. *Hell, I was the one going to need the iced water.*

"That won't be a problem," I looked at his sexy ass again. "I'll write you a check and get you that ice water now."

"Fine," he agreed, standing from the recliner.

Hypnotized, I watched as Kwame walked over to Bree, who was sitting at her finger fun table in her own little world—staring at the blocks and shaking her head back and forth violently.

"Goodbye, little one," he smiled down at her and playfully tugged one of her long pigtails before moving in front of me.

Kwame rose to stand way above me again. He had to be six foot four, and all of him was pure muscle.

I felt like a midget even though I was 5'9.

His gaze swept over me again quickly. Every bone in my body turned to liquid.

Kwame extended his large hand and this time, his gaze lingered.

By the time he walked outside, I felt under the influence. I went to the window and peeped out of the shades watching his muscles flexing as he lifted the equipment from his Ford pickup truck.

2

Mariah Carey's sultry voice was crooning "Vision Of Love." It was my ringtone. I almost cursed as I pulled my cellphone from my pocket. Who was this distracting me while I was watching Kwame cut my grass?

"Hey, girl."

"Hey, April," I grinned. "Are you ready for school Monday?"

"Girl, you know I am," April chuckled. "You and I are gonna have fun teaching fourth grade this year."

"I know that's right."

April and I had been friends since first grade. We'd lost touch senior year when April went to a different school, but met up again a couple of months ago. It was a few days before summer vacation began, and April was applying for a job at the same elementary school I worked at. Come Monday, I would be her Teacher's Assistant.

"So, what are you up to today?" I asked her.

"I'm trying to get settled into my new house."

"How do you like it?"

"This place is huge," April laughed. "As soon as I get settled in, I'm inviting you and Rich over for dinner to meet my husband."

"Oh, April that's so nice," I said, still eyeballing Kwame—who was riding his mower over the high grass. I opened the shades wider. Kwame had the nicest ass I'd ever seen, and with him sitting on the lawnmower...*Lord, have mercy.* Droplets of sweat began cascading down my face and between my breasts. I used my hands to fan myself.

"Did the landscaper come yet?" April asked.

"Yep, he's out there now cutting the grass. Why didn't you tell me he looked like that?"

"Like what?" April asked, clueless.

"Fine!" I whispered into the telephone.

April burst out laughing. "Why doesn't that surprise me? I see you still haven't changed from the boy crazy ways you had in high school. Now that you're a married woman, I thought you wouldn't pay him any attention."

"Girl, I'm not blind or dead. The man looks good, and he's nice."

"All of that is a plus, but did he give you a decent price on the yard?" April asked.

"Yeah, only fifty. Can you believe that?"

"Of course. I told him to look out for you or he was going to have to answer to me. I know Rich was happy with the price."

"Rich is asleep—as usual," I complained. "All he does is sleep. I'm telling you, this is not the marriage I dreamed of."

"Hang in there," April tried to encourage me.

"Easy for you to say," I joked. "Your husband just brought you a brand new house, and he took you to Florida for vacation a few weeks ago. I haven't been anyplace but this house the entire summer."

I sat on the ottoman next to the window and slouched forward, wishing I had April's life. She was married to an investment banker who bought her anything she wanted. April didn't have to work; said she did it because she loved teaching.

April let out a sympathetic sigh. "Don't be so hard on Rich. Things will get better."

"That's what you always say."

"It will."

"I hope so." I decided to stop venting. "If not, you'll hear about it."

April began laughing again. "I know that's right."

I laughed, too. April was a blessing in disguise. Since she'd entered my life again, I had someone to express all of my frustrations about

Rich to. In the two months' time she'd been back in town, I'd already told her all of my business. I stood and reopened the shades.

"I'm glad you're back, April. It's good to have someone to talk to."

"It's good to have you to talk to too," April sighed. "Well, let me get off this phone, girl. My hubby just walked in the door with Chinese food. Maybe I'll make him feed me with the chopsticks."

I smiled, even though I felt envious.

"See you Monday," I said before ending the call. Then I went back to staring at Kwame. I don't know how long I stood at that window lusting after him, but by the time I moved again I had to: he was finished with my yard and loading all of his equipment back onto the truck. I rushed to write his check–and get his glass of iced water. I poured an extra glass for myself because I needed one, too—badly.

~~~~

"Who the hell is you?" a grouchy, slurry voice stopped me from pouring Kwame another glass of ice water.

I placed the pitcher on the table and watched my sixty-three-year-old daddy, who everyone called Daddy Isaac, stroll into the living room. By the way his voice was slurring you would have thought he was drunk, but I knew better. The doctor told Daddy another shot of liquor would send him to sleep—for good. So it was no surprise when I noticed his gums were bare and his false teeth were missing.

I looked Daddy over to see if he was decent. He was wearing his cherry robe, but his gray hair was matted like he hadn't put a comb through it, and he had on a pair of worn bedroom shoes. Even though I'd brought him a new pair, he said he hated the way they felt and preferred the old ones better.

"Dad, this is Kw.."

"Kwame," he helped me pronounce his name correctly.

He smiled at my dad. Then at me.

"Well, what's he doing in here dripping sweat all over my hardwood floors?" Dad snapped.

He pulled his pipe from the pocket of his robe, walked to the deluxe recliner in the corner, and sat down.

"Kwame's gonna be taking care of the yard for us," I said, taking the empty glass from Kwame and placing it on the table.

"Did you bring a business license or any references I can take a look at, young man?"

"Dad," I said, cutting my eyes at him in disapproval, "he was referred by my best friend, April."

"I don't care if he was referred by Mother Teresa, I wanna see a business license or something in writing with a letterhead."

Kwame held up his hand. "I'll bring it on my next visit, sir."

"Good," Daddy declared, easing back in his recliner.

I looked at Kwame apologetically. He graced me with his gorgeous dimples.

"Sorry," I mouthed while giving him his check. "You have to excuse my dad; he's set in his ways."

"My grandfather in Ghana is the same way," Kwame chuckled, walking with me to the door.

"You're from Ghana?" I asked as I unlocked the screen door to let him out.

So that explained the African accent. I was more curious about him than ever.

"I was born and—"

"Kendra: how long a conversation you gonna have with the man?" Daddy grumbled. "And why you got that screen door open, letting them flies in here and all my cool air out?"

I shook my head as I followed Kwame outside into the furnace-like heat. Closing the door behind me, I couldn't help but feel embarrassed that my dad was treating me like I was six instead of twenty-four. Kwame and I walked side by side into the yard.

"Watch your step," Kwame warned, tugging me close to his side. My head landed against his chiseled chest. He smelt good—felt good. A chill raced up my spine and I forced myself to recover quickly.

"You almost stepped in that ant pile," he let me know, pointing it and two others out to me.

"I have two yards to cut in this area tomorrow. I'll stop by and get rid of them for you."

"How much?" I asked, still feeling my heart thrashing from his touch.

"Free. I wouldn't want your little one to get into those by accident."

"Thank you," I gushed.

It didn't make any sense how good-looking the man was. The impulse to shake my head as I watched him move away was powerful.

Kwame bowed his head and smiled as he strolled away, reminding me of a good dream that was slowly fading. I tried to remember every inch of his ripped body before he disappeared into his Ford truck and the tinted windows prevented me from seeing any further. Damn, this man was having an effect on me that I didn't understand. As he drove away, I got a flashback of his ass on the lawnmower and shivered. *Mysterious, sexy, and charismatic—the perfect combination,* I thought as I strolled back into the house and closed the door.

Standing in front of the door, I folded my arms across my chest and stared at Daddy, who had the same stubborn look on his face that he always did. Rich and I had been staying with my dad since the day we married. Drinking liquor half his life had my dad's liver hanging on by a string–at least, that's what the doctor told me. And unless Daddy had someone to look after him, he would have to go to a nursing home. So, instead of moving into our own house, me and Rich moved in with Daddy. And it had been pure hell every since.

"Daddy, do you have to be rude to everybody?" I complained.

Bree hadn't moved from the finger fun table—in fact, she was still staring into space—so I walked over to the couch so I could watch her.

"That man ain't nothing but trouble," Daddy replied, stuffing tobacco into his pipe and lighting it. "He looked like he got upset when I asked him for his business license, too."

"Stop being so paranoid. The man is harmless, and I hope you know you're not gonna find anyone else in their right mind that'll give us a price like he did." I glanced at my dad, then focused back on Bree. Using the bib around her neck, I wiped the drool from her mouth. "Every since you got sick, you think everyone is out to get you."

"It ain't got nothing to do with me being paranoid," Daddy argued while gumming on his pipe. "I seen the way that man looked at you. He trying to get next to you."

Daddy blew spicy smoke into the air.

"Oh, lord, Daddy; I'm married."

"Yeah, but do he know that?" my dad asked, leaning forward and staring at me.

His light brown skin looked even more wrinkled.

"Yes," I answered, rolling my eyes.

"What about you?"

"'What about me,' what?"

"You do know you made a vow to Rich. To love and behold him, forsaking all others…"

"Daddy, please, I've never cheated on Rich and I don't plan on starting."

"Then why you look so starry eyed."

"I'm not starry eyed," I snapped.

My dad was getting on my last nerve and it didn't help the affect Kwame was still having on me. Even though he was gone, his tangy cologne was still on my shirt. One whiff sent my heart racing. My head felt dreamy, and sweat glazed my forehead. I whipped my sweaty multicolored bangs behind my ears. I hadn't felt this turned on and alive since before I married Rich.

"I ain't ever seen you look this way over no man," my dad continued. "Not even when you brought Rich here to meet me for the first time. I hope you ain't getting no ideas in your head. You know how boy crazy you was in high school. Had a different boyfriend every week.

You a married woman, now. You can't have no boyfriend when you got a husband."

"You're making something out of nothing, Daddy."

"I hope to God I am. I just know that sometimes when you're having problems in your marriage, it's easy to fall for any man who comes along whispering sweet nothings in your ear."

"Who's having problems in their marriage?" I asked, looking right at my dad.

"You must think I was born today. You ain't talking to no fool or no baby. It ain't no secret you and Rich been having troubles."

"How do you know?" I wondered.

I never argued with Rich when Daddy was around. I wouldn't even frown or roll my eyes at him, even though I wanted to.

"I seen the way you treat him," my dad out-talked me. "You're cold. Plus, he's been sleeping in the den for almost a month."

"That don't have nothing to do with me," I grunted. "He just loves that 52-inch television in there."

"Nope, he just don't wanna hear your mouth."

I pulled Bree onto my lap, trying to calm her because she was shaking her head back and forth forcefully again.

"You got a good man 'round here," Daddy opened his newspaper. "Even though he don't do a lick of yard work and sleep most of the time, he's home—he's a good fellow. When you brought him here for the first time, I knew he was the one for you. I knew it."

I let out a weary breath. I was tired of Daddy telling me how good of a man Rich was. My head was starting to hurt. I stood to my feet then helped Bree up. It was time for her medicine; without it she would have brutal tantrums and bang her head into anything she could find. I thought our conversation was over, but my dad kept yacking.

"Alright," he said before I could walk away. "Don't let these words fall on deaf ears."

I turned to him and rolled my eyes. He was such a hypocrite. Daddy had cheated on my mama with any and everything that had breasts and hair between their legs, and now he was trying to school me.

Please.

"Well, I'm not you." I protested, rolling my neck.

"And what's that supposed to mean?" Daddy scooted to the edge of the recliner with the pipe hanging from his mouth.

"You know."

"No, go on and tell me."

"All I'm saying is: I will never cheat on my husband the way you cheated on Mama."

"Don't come starting that," Daddy warned.

He stood from the recliner, grabbed the newspaper, and tucked it under his arm. He looked hurt; ashamed.

"I ain't gonna sit here and listen to you like Rich do," he exclaimed. "You ain't gonna make me have no stroke."

"Then stop being a hypocrite; acting like you was a saint when you were married. You know that wasn't even the case."

Daddy stopped in front of me, his eyes nearly bulging from their sockets. "You speak on things you don't know nothing about."

"Oh, I know. You want me to go into details?" I snapped, grabbing Bree's hand. I wanted to say more but Dad shuffled into the kitchen and damned near landed on the opened dishwasher door.

"Damn it, Kendra. What I told you about leaving the dishwasher open. Then you got those knives sticking up inside it. One day somebody gonna slip and kill themselves on that thing."

Suddenly I felt bad about Daddy almost slipping, and about the way I just argued with

him. I went to the dishwasher and closed the
door. I wanted to apologize to Daddy, too. But
he walked away quicker than I'd seen him
move in a long time, dismissing the argument
by slamming his bedroom door.

3

As usual, Rich didn't come to bed that night. He finally woke up at five that evening. Then his best friend, Cory—who everyone called Tongue Tied Cory because he talked like his tongue was stuck to the root of his mouth—came over with some new Xbox games. The two of them spent the entire night playing Xbox, eating up everything in the kitchen and watching television. I didn't say anything. At least he was taking Bree and me out the next day.

As I settled against the king-sized pillows on my platform bed I tried to sleep, but all I could think about was Kwame: his beautiful African accent, gorgeous body, and magnetic personality. He'd been so attentive, too—protecting me from the ant piles. Kwame knew how to validate me. Small things, like what he'd done yesterday, meant a lot. I liked attention—no, I loved attention—and this man knew how to shower me with it. I wondered if he was married. I hadn't seen a ring on his finger, but that didn't mean anything.

Rich didn't wear one either—said it irritated his fingers. Maybe Kwame didn't wear one because of his job. One thing was for sure: a fine man like that had a woman somewhere, and whoever she was, she was luckier than someone who'd hit the jackpot twice in one day.

~~~~

The next morning, I got up early. The sun was splashing yellow all over my flowered-paper walls, and the birds were chirping happily outside my bedroom window. I hadn't slept well, and the noise Rich and Cory made half the night didn't have a thing to do with it. I'd dreamed about Kwame. We were making love—no, having rough sex in my living room. And he was hitting it hard—doing everything I yearned for to my body, getting me hot enough to pop like a fire cracker, teasing all my hot spots: my breasts, neck, and ears…pleasing me like he knew my body better than I did. I woke up sweating and moaning. My clitoris was throbbing so hard, I was on the verge of an orgasm. One stroke down there would have sent me into spasms. I sat on the edge of my platform bed, squeezed my legs together, and took a couple of deep breaths to pull myself together.

If Rich had been in the bedroom I would have thrown him down on the bed and tore him up just to release this pressure in me. I didn't know what it was about Kwame: he was affecting me like no man ever had. For the first time in years,

I felt butterflies. I was flowing again; feeling things I hadn't since the day Rich slipped that ring on my finger and we began living our dull, simple lives together. I shook Kwame from my head, but my body still called for him. I decided to take a shower. Reaching over, I adjusted the water. Already the temperature outside was in the upper 90s. I wanted to head to the beach. Bree would love the water, the sand and the salty air. We'd never taken her and I knew this would be a good getaway before she and I both started school tomorrow.

After I showered, I put on my ruffled top and a jean mini skirt: just the type of attire a teacher wouldn't wear. I didn't want to look like no educator today. I wanted to look hot. I wanted to have fun and feel young. Hell, I was young. I was twenty-four and I was gonna act my age. I slipped into my sandals and took an hour to curl my colorful weave. When I was done, I examined myself. I thought I looked cute—no, I knew I looked cute. I put ribbons in Bree's hair and dressed her up, too. After the beach, I wanted us to go out to dinner on the strip. Maybe I'd wear a two piece bathing suit; I had a hot pink one in the closet. Rich might pay more attention to me if he saw other men on the beach gawking at me. I smiled at the thought.

I flew down the stairs to wake Rich up, but he was nowhere in the house. I looked outside; his Ford F-150 was gone, too. This had to be a mistake. Maybe he just ran to the store or something.

In the living room, Daddy was looking at himself in the mirror above the fireplace. Since he was spending the day at his sister Sherry's house, Daddy was dressed in his khaki slacks and a white dress shirt. His hair was combed and his false teeth were sparkling in his mouth.

"You look good," I let him know. "I'm glad to see you getting out of the house instead of staying upstairs in your room."

He just grunted.

"Daddy, you seen Rich?" I asked next, going over to brush a piece of lint from his shirt.

"He told me to tell you he'd be back this evening."

Daddy looked me up and down quickly.

"That skirt you got on is too short," he noted gruffly, "but my grandbaby sure looks pretty."

He smiled at Bree, who was sitting on the sofa staring into space and shaking a rattle in her hands. "Where you going?" he asked me.

"We were supposed to be going to the beach with Rich," I muttered.

I went into the family room so my dad wouldn't hear me. Snatching up the house phone I dialed Rich's cell. I was gonna cuss him out but the call went straight to voicemail. I was so mad, I was trembling. My eyes started stinging. Just then Daddy called for me, so I pulled myself together before walking back into the living room. Daddy was looking at me like he felt sorry for me, or maybe he just wanted to make up for our spat yesterday. Whatever it was, I didn't want any sympathy.

"Why don't you get out of this house today?" my dad suggested. "Come over to my sister Sherry's with me. She's cooking Sunday dinner."

He put on his hat.

"Daddy, you know I can't stand Aunt Sher ry," I admitted, shoulders slumping. "And I hope you ain't going over there to drink because you know that's all Aunt Sherry does."

"I ain't took a swallow in years," Daddy reminded me, running his tongue across his false teeth. "Why would I start now?"

At the sound of a horn blowing I looked out the shades. It was Aunt Sherry's family van pulling into the driveway. Don't know why I expected it to be Rich.

"Well, at least let my grandbaby come with me," Dad grabbed Bree's hand.

"Okay, but you'd better keep your eyes on her," I ordered him right before I bent down and gave Bree a hug.

"Child, I've been taking care of babies before you were born. I raised you alright, didn't I?"

I put Bree's name tag around her neck with our address and my cell phone number on it, just in case she wandered away—which she'd done before. I packed her medicine then helped her out to the van with my dad.

"I'll bring them back tonight, honey," Aunt Sherry said before pulling out of the driveway. I waved to them and watched until the car was gone. It was so pretty outside it looked dream-like. I looked around the close-knit neighbor-hood I'd been raised in. Everyone's car was gone. I must have been the only one at home. Slowly I turned and went back into the dead house. My day was ruined. I picked up the phone and called Rich at least twelve more times; each time I got his voicemail.

"I'm done with him," I mumbled. I wanted to cry, but held it in. Instead, I flopped down on the loveseat, talking to myself and generally feeling miserable. The urge to cuss Rich out was so strong it gave me the shakes. Before I married

Rich I had a life—friends; and had gone on lots of trips. I always had men taking me out and buying me things. My life had been exciting.

Now I felt like a dog tied to a tree.

4

An hour later, Rich finally decided to call back. I jumped up from the loveseat with the telephone in my hand.

"What happened?" I hollered at him. "I thought you said you were gonna take me and Bree out today."

"Cory had an extra ticket to the BSC basketball game," Rich said nonchalantly. "He wanted me to go with him."

"Oh, so you just left without telling me?"

"I told your dad."

"Don't play stupid. You should have told me. But you didn't because you knew what you promised me yesterday."

There was loud chattering in the background. Girls cheering. People laughing. Horns blaring. Rich was having a good time. Which made me even more heated because I was stuck in the house.

"Why don't you go out without me?" Rich suggested.

"You're missing the point!" Sitting on the arm of the loveseat I clutched the phone while trying my best to calm down. "When you make a promise, you're supposed to keep it. But Rich always looks out for Rich. I don't even know why I'm talking to you. Talking to you is like talking to a wall. You never listen to me. Never. You do what you want to do."

I could hear Rich breathing hard. I wanted him to get upset. I wanted to ruin his day just like he'd ruined mine.

"Come on, Kendra," Rich griped. "I work six days a week. I only get Sundays off. I want to enjoy it. I don't want to spend it listening to you complain all day."

"I complain because you never do anything with me!" I shouted so loud my eyes felt like they would explode out of my head.

Rich let out a grunt, and my anger doubled.

"Man, I'm tired of this shit," I blasted. "When I try to spend time with you, you'd rather sleep or play video games with Cory. What about me? When do I get some of your time, huh?"

"I don't have to do everything with you," Rich fumed back. "You have friends. You could have gone places without me. No one made you stay home this entire summer."

"That's the problem," I stood from the love-seat again. "You don't do anything with me or Bree. You'd rather spend time with Cory than with us. You must be sleeping with him."

"I'm hanging up," Rich mumbled into the line. "You acting real childish right now."

"You know what?" I almost sobbed. "I give up, Rich. I give up on you. On us. If you won't pay attention to me, some other man will. So go on and have fun. Do you, 'cause I'ma do me!"

"Whatever," Rich sounded like he didn't care. "I'll see you tonight."

He hung up.

I called Rich again but it went straight to voicemail on the first ring. My emotions were all over the place. The room was cutting cartwheels, or at least it looked that way. I slammed the telephone down and stormed into the family room, looking for something important of his to destroy. My eyes fell on his Xbox. I snatched it so hard the plug snapped from the socket. Rich had just purchased that Xbox from Walmart and it cost him a pretty good penny. I also grabbed the case with all his games in it—including the new game Cory just brought over last night.

Outside, in the distance, I could hear equipment buzzing and smell wet grass. Someone was doing yard work next door. Kwame appeared from the side of the neighbor's house, sweating, with a weed whacker in his hands. As our eyes locked, my heart started beating a little faster. On some strange level I didn't quite understand, he and I connected. Waves and smiles were exchanged. My entire mood shifted. Kwame was a drug. Better than Percocet, Vicodin or Prozac. Still staring at him, I quickly tossed the Xbox, the games—everything—into the trash. Suddenly, my toes and legs began stinging. Shit, they were on fire! Looking down, I saw I had stepped into a huge ant pile. Fire ants swarmed my bare legs and feet. I jumped out of the ant pile screaming, trying to get them off, but the ants were everywhere.

"Kendra!" Kwame called out, covering the short distance between us in two or three leaps. He snatched his shirt off and, twirling it around, swatted at my legs over and over; except it seemed like the more he tried to brush the ants off, the worse the stinging became. Scooping me into his arms, Kwame cradled me gently and rushed into my house.

"Is your father or husband home?" he asked.

I told him no.

He looked panicked.

"Where is your bathroom?" was his next question.

"The next door on the left," I hissed in pain.

In a flash, Kwame ran down the hall. He sat me on the edge of the tub and placed my legs under cool running water.

"You're going to be okay," he assured me as he began vigorously massaging my legs.

Minutes later all of the ants were off and floating in the water.

"How do you feel?" Kwame asked, his heavy African drawl bouncing off the walls.

"Like my flesh is on fire," I whimpered.

Kwame lathered his large hands with soap and began massaging my legs again. I tried my best to ignore the enticing heat of his hands. Staring at Kwame on his knees, with his shirt off, kneading my legs, I thought: *Lord have mercy, this man is beautiful.* I greedily consumed his twelve pack stomach, chiseled calves, buff biceps and triceps, ripped back and tight ass. *Let me pluck my mind from this runaway train,* I thought to myself, *before Kwame notices my eyes eating away at his flesh.* He let the water out of the tub, reached for the towel and began gently patting my legs dry.

"So tell me, what are you doing home alone on a gorgeous day like this, anyway?"

"You'd have to ask my husband that," I grumbled. "Maybe he'll tell you why he prefers to spend more time at work or with his friend Cory than with me. I guess it's just a man thing."

"Man thing?" he looked confused. "I think not."

"So, you would spend a day like this with your wife instead of working or hanging out with your friends?"

"If I had a wife, yes."

If he had a wife. You've gotta be kidding me, I thought. I just knew this fine man had a woman—or women—all over town. I was about to probe further but Kwame changed the course of the conversation.

"I should have come here first and gotten rid of the fire ants for you like I'd planned yesterday, then this wouldn't have happened." he grieved, looking at me with those gray eyes of his.

"This was not your fault. I should have looked where I was going," I muttered, thinking what a bitch Karma was. I'd thrown Rich's game away and got hurt in the process.

"But it is my fault," Kwame insisted, resting his hand on my leg lightly. "I'm your yardman and anything that is wrong with your yard is my fault."

His hand grazed my breast as he placed the towel back onto the rack. A shiver rushed up my spine.

"Are you sure you're okay?" Kwame voiced his concerned.

I had to play it off. "Yeah…uh… I just hate ants, snakes and anything that crawls."

"Well, you'd better stay inside until after I treat your yard." He smiled again, showing his dimples. "I chopped the head off of snake this morning over at your neighbor's."

"Snake?" I squirmed at the thought.

"Yeah, I'm putting sulfur around you and your neighbor's houses."

"I don't know how you can stand snakes. Ants…worms…spiders…" My voice trailed off and I frowned.

"Growing up in Ghana, I was surrounded by snakes, geckos, praying mantises, and ants five times bigger than those tiny ones that attacked you." Kwame rose to his feet. "I'm used to living in the wild," he winked at me before asking for the rubbing alcohol.

My index finger directed Kwame toward the cabinet.

~~~~

I was drooling as he walked away. *Girl, quit acting like you ain't never seen a fine man before,* I demanded myself.

Kwame gathered me into his arms again, then sat me on the toilet. I was in heaven being catered to in this manner. Gently, he began slathering my legs with the alcohol. The coolness of the alcohol made my body tingle.

"Should I stop?" Kwame asked.

"I'm fine," I almost moaned. "This feels so good."

I lowered my eyes to meet Kwame's. He held my gaze. Finally I had to look away: the energy between us could start a fire.

"Who is that?" he asked, nodding his head toward the picture that sat on the shelf.

"My mother," I said, smiling.

"Ah, so that's who you inherited your beauty from," he said in his sexy African tenor. "Your mother is very beautiful, just like you."

Our eyes connected again; my heart stopped beating. Kwame's gaze slowly traveled from my face to my long shapely legs then back up, stopping at my thighs because of the miniskirt I sported. He got a good, long look before his eyes reached mine again. Surprisingly, I didn't feel embarrassed or uncomfortable: I felt turned on by the starved look in his eyes.

"My mother was very beautiful," I stuttered weakly. I had to force myself to speak. "She left my dad and me when I was six. Less than a year later, she died from a drug overdose.

Kwame looked at me with both pity and shock. I didn't want him looking at me like that, and I didn't want to talk about my mother and how she died, either.

"So, you told me you were from Ghana?" I changed the subject.

"I lived there until I was thirteen," he said, rubbing more alcohol onto my legs. "Then my father took me and my brother and we immigrated here."

"And your mother?"

His gaze turned sad. "She stayed behind. She died a few years later."

We stared at each other again. Connected in that way. Kwame touched my chin lightly.

"Different countries, same experience," he whispered.

Electric sparks started flying again. My head was swooning.

"I need to get some ice for your legs. Where is your kitchen?"

"Down the hall, you won't miss it."

I smiled to myself at the sheer pleasure of watching Kwame's well-developed rear end as he walked away.

~~~~

My cell phone began vibrating. It was Rich.

"What do you want?"

"You cooled down yet?"

I sucked my teeth.

"You take everything I say as a game, don't you?" I asked.

"I'll be home soon," Rich responded, ignoring my question completely.

"And?"

"I'm taking you and Bree out for an hour or two."

"I don't give a rat's ass if you do or if you don't," I said nonchalantly. I closed the cell phone just in time to see Kwame strolling back with a Ziploc bag full of ice.

"You must keep this icepack on your legs for at least fifteen minutes to prevent swelling."

"Okay," I agreed.

Kwame towered over me looking like an African Prince.

"Do you want to go into the living room?" he asked.

"Yes." I stood and attempted to take a few steps.

"Let me carry you," he offered.

Who could refuse an offer like that? For the third time that day, Kwame hoisted me in his powerful arms.

The blood began racing beneath my skin, heating it as our eyes locked and then froze onto each other's.

I could feel Kwame's heart jack hammering against the hard wall of his chest.

For a moment, I felt this strange impulse to kiss him. I bit my lip to stop the foolish notion. Was I crazy? I'd just met this man yesterday.

Kwame cleared his throat and blinked as if he was coming out of a trance.

I couldn't help but think he'd been pondering the same thing I had. I was on fire—and not my legs—but in between those bad boys was an inferno blazing out of control.

"Didn't you tell me you liked roses?" Kwame asked.

"Like? I love them," I replied, trying to control my breathing. "Why?"

"Well, I have some rosebushes in my truck that I uprooted from a clinic's yard. It would be a waste to take them to the dumpster. Why don't I plant them here for you after I take care of the ant piles?"

"That would be nice," I said, forcing myself to stop giggling.

It impressed me that Kwame had actually listened to me yesterday and that he remembered what I said about loving roses.

This man was incredible: a diamond in the rough.

His eyes stayed super-glued onto mine as he placed me gently onto the couch.

His face was so close I could smell his minty breath and Polo cologne.

I felt the impulse to kiss Kwame's plump lips again, and to run the tip of my tongue across his frosty white teeth, but the front door unlocked, interrupting us.

5

Daddy and Bree strode inside, along with the one-hundred-plus degree heat. Daddy looked at the both of us—mostly at Kwame's bare, beefy chest.

Kwame bolted upright and cleared his throat.

"What in the hell is going on up in here?" Daddy roared like a grizzly bear on the warpath. He grabbed Bree's hand and hurried over to us.

"What are you doing back here?" I demanded; pissed off that he had interrupted us.

"Every goodbye ain't gone and every closed eye ain't sleep," Daddy answered.

He sat Bree down next to me.

"What's going on?" he asked again.

"Daddy, calm down," I insisted. A migraine burned behind my eyes. "Nothing is going on. I got into an ant pile. Kwame helped me."

"That's all well and good," my dad said, looking first at my blistered legs, then looking Kwame up and down. "But why is your shirt off, young man?"

"I left it outside," Kwame informed him, looking so nervous and embarrassed I felt sorry for him.

"Daddy, he used his shirt to get the ants off me."

"Well, he need to get outta here and go outside and put it back on. Show some respect," Daddy put his foot down. "And did you bring that business license?"

"I forgot, sir," Kwame shifted from one foot to the other. "I'll bring it next time."

"Uh huh," my dad huffed, keeping his eyes on Kwame, who rushed outside the house so quickly I didn't have time to thank him.

"I don't like this," Dad continued, shaking his head. "I don't like this at all, Kendra."

"Daddy, please. Not today," I warned him.

I pulled Bree onto my lap and looked her in her eyes but she didn't look at me. She never looked me or anyone else in their eyes. I kissed her on her chubby cheek. Then I focused on my dad, who was still looking at the slightly ajar door Kwame slipped out of.

"What are you doing back early anyway? You just left two hours ago."

"My old low down dirty sister Sherry invited Raymond over for dinner," Daddy grumbled.

He shuffled over to his favorite recliner and sat down.

"Uncle Raymond's back in town?"

My eyes lit up like fireworks. Uncle Raymond was my favorite uncle, and I hadn't seen him since I was little.

"Yeah; he's back. I made Sherry bring me home."

"Daddy, I don't know why you hate Uncle Raymond so much. Ever since I was a little girl, you two been going at it."

"And for the little years I have left, we gonna go at it," Dad said sharply. "He wanted to come over here and see you but I told him no. He ain't welcome at my house."

"You've got some nerve," I countered. "If you don't wanna see Uncle Raymond, that's you; but you won't stop me from talking to him."

"No, I can't stop you from talking to him no more that I can stop you from flirting with that yardman outside."

"His name is Kwame," I told him.

"Kwan…Kwame…whatever the hell it is, I don't care! I don't want that man in this house when I'm not here. It looks bad. You're a married woman. Have more respect for yourself— your husband. What would the neighbors think?"

I was about to say something smart to my dad but the door opened again and in walked Rich and his tongue-tied friend, Cory.

~~~~

I let out a grunt and closed my eyes. It was no secret that I didn't like Cory. He was always hanging up under Rich, and on top of that he was constantly badmouthing me to Rich and putting ideas in Rich's head.

Cory looked just as bad as he talked. His shoulder length dreads looked like they hadn't been washed in centuries and he had acne all over his face. I rolled my eyes so hard they almost got stuck. Cory said hello to my dad and went to the family room—probably to play the game. *Not today he won't. He'd better go get it from the trash can.* I smirked at the thought.

"Kendra, what happened to you?" Rich asked.

He pulled off his shades and walking over to me, his bow legs very apparent in those jeans he was sporting.

"She got ate up by them ants out in the yard, boy," Daddy informed Rich. Gripping the stem tightly between his false teeth, he lit his pipe. "Son, you need to spend more time with your wife."

"That's what I came home to do, Pops."

"Then why Cory with you?"

Daddy pulled his pipe from his mouth and stared at Rich.

"Yeah, why is he with you?" I repeated, rolling my eyes again.

"He came to get his game."

I smiled to myself. Cory came back into the room and stood beside Rich.

"The game is gone," Cory wailed, dragging his hands through his dreads.

"Gone?" Rich raised his eyebrows. "Pops, did you borrow it?"

"You know I don't like them games," Dad sneered. Grabbing the remote he flipped on the television.

"Kendra, did you move it?" Rich asked.

"I threw it in the trash," I said indifferently.

"You what?!" Cory and Rich bellowed in unison. Both were staring at me like I was a fool.

"I didn't stutter," I jeered at them. "Your games are in the trash."

"This some bullshit," Cory stamped his foot.

His heavy tongue made him barely intelligible.

Daddy just shook his head and continued puffing on his pipe and watching television.

"Why'd you do that?" Rich demanded.

"Because you care more about that stupid game than about me."

"Man, I swear you're childish," Rich said through clenched teeth.

Cory looked me up and down, frowning his nose at me before stomping out the door to go get their precious Xbox from the trash can.

"What sense does that make to throw my games away?" Rich growled at me. "You're gonna pay for anything that's ruined."

"We'll see," I snapped.

The telephone began ringing and Daddy answered it.

"It's for you," he told Rich.

Rich took the receiver and talked for about five minutes, but the only part of the conversation I heard was: "How many days do you need me to stay out of town?"

I looked at Rich, not believing the words that had just rolled off his tongue.

"Out of town," I muttered, snorting like a bull. I knew it was his job calling.

Rich hung up the phone and sauntered slowly back to me.

"The job needs me for a few days," he said, inserting himself between Bree and me. "There were some bad twisters in North Carolina last night and a lot of people's power is out. I'm leaving tonight."

Scoffing, I folded my arms across my chest. Daddy looked at Rich and shook his head.

"Do you really have to go? It ain't good to be away from your family so much, son. You ain't hurting for money so you don't have to work as hard as you do."

"They need me," Rich replied, pulling Bree onto his lap.

"So does your wife," Daddy shot back. "I came home today and the yardman was in here tending to her."

"Tending to her?!" Rich looked at me then out the window at Kwame who was spraying insecticide over the ant piles.

I didn't bother to explain the story to Rich, but Dad did. Not that Rich cared anyway. He didn't have a jealous bone in his body. It would have felt good to see him jealous, though. At least I'd know he cared. But just like I thought, the conversation about Kwame died out quicker than a flash of lighting.

"Well, it looks like we can't go out now, Kendra," Rich said, looking at my swollen legs. He kissed Bree on the forehead.

"I bet you're happy," I snarled. Rising from my seat I grabbed my daughter's hand.

Rich tried to catch my arm, but I snatched it away.

"Bree starts school tomorrow and you're not gonna be here, as usual."

I made sure not to raise my voice in front of my dad. Lifting Bree into my arms, I walked away.

"You see, I can't talk to you when you're like this," Rich said, following me.

Cory came back in the house with the Xbox in one hand and the case of games in the other. "Man, our game is ruined. Water or some kind of juice got on it."

He cut his eyes at me, shoulders sagging lower than his jeans. "Some of these games fell out the case and got all scratched up, too."

Cory held up his new game for Rich to see.

"Good," I snapped.

"Kendra!" Rich shouted, looking confused and angry. "What's up with you today? Now I gotta buy another Xbox." He turned back to Cory. "Don't worry about it, man," he promised. "I'll replace it."

I tried to leave the room again but this time Rich seized my wrist.

"Why are doing crazy shit like this? What's wrong with you?" he shouted.

"You know what's wrong with me, so don't play dumb."

"Let's go in the room and talk."

"No: just pack your shit and leave," I hissed. "Your job needs you."

We stared each other down for a few seconds. Then Rich walked away.

An hour later he was gone.

6

The next morning, I took my time driving Bree to school. My legs were blistered pretty badly from the ant bites but I had to do what I had to do. I left for work early, so I had plenty of time. I could tell Bree wasn't happy about the change in routine. Like most children who suffered from autism, she hated inconsistencies in her schedule. Even though she couldn't talk, she communicated by banging her head when she was upset. At the moment, Bree was banging it on the car window. I pulled her up so she wouldn't hurt herself, and she began whipping her head up and down hella hard—moaning in between. Damn. I hoped the medicine I'd given her that morning kicked in soon.

It was times like these that I really needed Rich to support me. Since the day we found out Bree had Autism, Rich had been emotionally absent for her. I knew he felt guilty. Sometimes I did too. I was the one who carried Bree in my womb for nine months. I hadn't drank, smoked or even been around anything that smelled toxic. I had taken good care of myself, yet my baby girl still had Autism. But, I had to remind myself that it wasn't our fault. The doctor told us autism was still a puzzle, and research was being done every day. He said some of it could be due to genetics, and the other: environment. Then he told us Bree would be dependent on family for the remainder of her life. She would never be normal. Bullshit. Anything was possible. I worked with Bree the entire summer doing therapy, even though it seemed like she wasn't registering anything I told her. Unlike Rich, though, I remained hopeful.

My cell began vibrating. It was Rich, so I decided not to answer it. Rich had called last night to let me know he made it to North Carolina. I could care less. Rich cared more about work than about me and Bree.

I pulled into Dawson Special Education Center and grabbed Bree's book bag. I was happy to have found a school that catered only to autistic children. My dream was to one day open up a private daycare for autistic kids. I had already looked into a building I wanted on the south side of town that would be perfect. I walked Bree to her classroom and met her teachers. To my surprise, Bree didn't act out when I kissed her and told her goodbye. It made me feel a lot better. Fifteen minutes later, when I arrived at Creekside Elementary School, no one but my friend April was in our classroom. April was setting up name tags for our new students. She and I hugged each other and went on and on about how good the other looked.

"Girl, that collar dress you have on is nice," April said.

I smiled, looking at the Blue Lagoon Mandarin dress I sported.

"And you are wearing that blonde hair," I complemented her in return.

April gave me a dismissive wave and handed me the remainder of the name tags when I told her she looked pretty but I really meant it. Not many Black women with Hershey-chocolate skin like April's could pull the blonde look off, but April was rocking it.

"Can you put the rest of those name tags on the desks before the kids get here?" April asked before striding to the chalk board to write the word Welcome.

April had eczema, and the left side of her face, both her arms, neck, and even her legs broke out in dry patches off and on. On top of that, she had a lazy eye that she tried to conceal by wearing her blonde bangs long. To make matters worse, April had no shape. She was dried up like a raisin—no hips, no behind, and a flat chest like a boy. But her clothes were top quality. Plus she always had on nice jewelry. Her wrist and fingers were shining big time. I looked at the big wedding rock on her hand, envious, then moved around the room placing the remaining name tags on the desks.

"So, what's going on with you and Rich?" April asked, glancing back at me.

I told her everything that had happened yesterday, leaving out the part about Kwame.

"I don't think me and Rich are gonna make it."

Just saying that out loud made me feel shitty.

"If it wasn't for Bree, I would have been done left him," I continued.

My eyes got all misty as I thought about how I didn't want to break up my family. When my mother and father split, I was messed up. I wouldn't wish that feeling on my worst enemy. Certainly not on Bree.

April came over to me. She took the name tags from my hand and straightened out the ones I had already placed on the desks. I shook my head, knowing she was a perfectionist. Had always been that way.

"What you need to do when Rich comes back into town is talk to him. You guys have been together for a long time. Don't throw it away."

"I tried talking to that fool, but he doesn't listen," I spat. "I might as well talk to a brick wall."

"There must have been something about him you loved; you married him. What are the man's good qualities?" April asked, her lazy eye wandering as she looked at me.

I tried to think of something, but I couldn't remember a thing. The only thing I had in my head was how he worked all the time, so I told her that.

"You know, most women wished the only complaint they had about their man was that he worked too much." April folded her arms across her chest and smiled.

"Yeah, until they trade places with me and walk in my shoes," I muttered.

A knock on the door interrupted us. Standing in the doorway with a crystal vase full of assorted flowers was a delivery man.

"Delivery for April," he announced, holding out an electronic device for her to sign.

I followed April to the door. She signed the electronic pad then thanked the delivery man. Looking at the card, April read aloud.

"Thinking of you. Have a good first day of school. Love you always, Your husband, Andrew."

I shook my head.

"Man, April, you're lucky to have a good husband," I told her, feeling hella jealous again.

Maybe I was missing out. Maybe there was a man out there who could fulfill me and treat me just as good as April's husband treated her.

"Speaking of my husband Andrew," April said, face all lit up as she set the flowers on top of the bookshelf, "he wanted me to invite you and Rich over for dinner next week."

"Thanks April, but now wouldn't be a good time. I can't stand Rich. I don't want to go anyplace with him."

April looked disappointed.

"Well then, have drinks with me and my husband tomorrow night at Passion's Restaurant."

"I don't know."

"Come on. I'd hate for you to be at home alone and angry."

"Oh, alright," I gave in. "What time?"

"Seven," April said, walking back to her desk. "And when I'm done decorating my house, I want you to come over and take a look at it."

"You know I will. Just let me know when. I know your house is beautiful," I replied, trying to sound happy.

"It is. It has four bedrooms, three baths and a pool out back," April exclaimed.

Outside I was smiling, but inside I was green with envy. April had made something out of herself. And to think she had been the one raised in foster care and constantly picked on in school, while I had been raised by my father who spoiled me rotten, and was voted Most Popular and Most Likely To Succeed. *Well, look at me now: married to an inattentive husband, working as a Teacher's Assistant, and still living at home with Daddy*, I thought.

April must have noticed the depressed look on my face because she stopped talking. She reached underneath her desk and handed me a gift bag.

"What's this?" I asked, surprised.

"Look inside," she urged with a giggle.

I reached in and pulled out a name plate with my name on it.

"It's real gold!" April beamed.

"I can see that," I responded, eyes wide and breathless. "But, I didn't get you anything."

"That's okay," April continued to smile. "Just keep being my friend."

She put my nameplate on my desk: the small one that was next to her large one.

"Oh, believe me, I will," I promised, pulling April into a tight hug.

We heard a knock on the door. A parent stood outside with a child. I walked with April to the door to welcome the student to the fourth grade.

~~~~

I was as excited as a little child on Halloween when I walked into Passion's Restaurant the next night. Rich and I never went anyplace special, supposedly because he was trying to save money. Rich didn't want to work at the electric company his whole life, just like I damned sure didn't want to be a Teacher's Assistant for the rest of mine's. We both had dreams. Big Dreams. Rich wanted to open his own truck driving company and I wanted to open that private daycare for autistic children. So the sacrifice was: we never went anyplace fancy and we saved every penny. Rich never wanted to go anyplace anyway, but if we did, we'd go to McDonalds or K-mart: some corny shit like that. We never went to cushy restaurants or anyplace extravagant. This was a big deal to me, so I took it all in.

Passion's Restaurant was off the chain! First off, you couldn't get in unless you had reservations, and a dress code was in full effect. No sneakers. No casual dress wear. My stilettos clicked on the marble floor as I strode to the reservations booth. All eyes were on me and the way my scoop-necked sheath dress was hugging my thick, toned hips. *If only Rich's eyes were as filled with desire as the eyes of the men in this restaurant rubbernecking at me,* I thought. I needed that to feel like he still cared, that he still wanted me.

"I'm a guest of April," I told the dirty-blonde, freckle-faced hostess.

"Oh yes, right this way," she said, leading me through the elegant restaurant. April had it going on if she could afford expensive restaurants like this. I took in the round tables, cushioned chairs and elaborate candles atop each table. The hostess seated me in the back at a secluded table near a band playing jazz onstage. Couples were swaying their hips on the dance floor to the slow tune the band was performing.

April and her husband hadn't arrived yet. I was nervous about meeting April's husband. After all, he was a big time investment banker. He and April lived in a mansion. April drove a Benz. Wore clothes I couldn't afford and jewelry that would take months of my salary to pay for. So, I could only imagine that her husband was the best. I wouldn't be surprised if she walked in with Denzel. While I waited, I called Daddy to check on Bree. I was glad he'd kept her for me. It felt good to be out of the house and back around people again. When I ended the call less than ten minutes later, April still wasn't there.

I called April on her cell and got no answer, so I texted her, asking where she was.

—HURRY UP AND GET HERE, GIRL, I typed quickly then pressed send.

"Kendra?"

My heart missed a few beats. Without looking up, I knew why.

"Kwame?!" I asked, only it was more of a statement. He was dressed up. Sharp as shit. Black slacks, gold and black collared shirt, gold watch, and dress shoes. It amazed me how he could look so delectable in either work or dress attire. The clothes didn't bring out Kwame— Kwame brought out the clothes.

"What are you doing here?" I asked, sounding like the wind had gotten knocked out of me. It sure felt that way.

"I was meeting with a client, but he canceled," Kwame informed me, shoving his hands in his slacks and looking down on me with his spellbinding gaze. "You must be dining with your husband?"

Kwame looked around the restaurant quickly like he was searching for Rich. I couldn't help but stare at him, he was so fine!

"No, I'm supposed to be having drinks with my best friend April and her husband."

The dirty-blonde, freckle-faced hostess interrupted us.

"April called. It looks like she won't be able to make it. Her husband got sick on the way."

"Is he alright?" I worried.

"Oh, yes. She said it's most likely stomach issues. She wants you to order whatever you want. The drinks and food are on her."

The host gave me a thousand-watt smile before rushing away.

I looked up at Kwame. *This was perfect,* I thought. *A little too perfect—like it was meant for us to meet up here tonight.*

"Well, having drinks with my best friend and her husband is out," I said, raising both eyebrows.

"Would you mind if I joined you? Unless…"

"Sit down," I ordered with a laugh. I patted the spot on the table in front of me. "Any man who saved me from being eaten alive by ants is welcomed to dine with me."

Kwame grinned in return, his dimples deepening. It made him even more gorgeous. He didn't hesitate to sit all six feet four inches of his luscious flesh in the seat across from mine's.

I cleared my throat and met his eyes.

"First off, let me tell you how sorry I am for the way my father treated you yesterday."

Kwame held up his hand to halt me.

"Kendra, it didn't bother me. The only thing that mattered was that you were okay," he said sincerely. "How do your legs feel, by the way?"

His eyes slid down to one of my bare legs, sticking out from under the table.

"A little blister's here and there, but nothing I can't handle," I replied.

The mesmerized look in his eyes as he continued staring at my leg brought goose bumps to my flesh. Clearing his throat, Kwame shook his head like he was clearing away a fog of some kind then refocused on me.

"Then you won't mind going outside on the balcony with me," he said, fanning his shirt in and out. "It's less stuffy than in here."

He stood and helped me from my chair, placing a massive hand on my back. The smell of his cologne had me lava hot. I wondered how those hands would feel all over me. Trembling slightly, I struggled to pull myself together.

"So tell me, what are the drinks like here?" I asked as we walked through the crowd.

"They are as delicious as you are beautiful," Kwame replied, his sexy eyes roaming little by little over my body.

"Yeah, right," I laughed, pretending Kwame's flirting had no effect on me.

"That's not a line. It's a compliment," he noted, opening the balcony door and letting me pass through first. "You need to learn how to accept them."

"Oh, I know how to accept them; it's just that I haven't heard one in so long."

"I don't believe that," Kwame responded, looking me up and down slowly again like he was stripping me naked.

"It's the truth," I revealed, big grin on my face. "But anyway, thanks for the compliment."

We moved into the secluded 1400 square-foot terrace, complete with its own bar, white and red couches, and a karaoke machine. The air was warm and dark, making the terrace seem sensual, sophisticated and mysterious: just like Kwame. Shit, I silently wished I wasn't married.

"So, I guess you have drinks here often?" I asked.

"Only when I meet with clients."

"This place is nice," I noted, taking in the incredible panoramic view and the skyline. "It's the type of place you'd take someone special; like a fiancée, girlfriend... even your children."

Just then, Kwame came to a stop at a table near the bar.

"I don't have a wife, girlfriend, fiancée or children," he said, pulling out my chair for me. "But you do have a husband," his dimples deepened. "So, where is he tonight?"

After Kwame pushed my chair in, he leaned over me and looked directly into my eyes.

"Out of town working, as usual," I turned my gaze away from his.

"Lucky me," Kwame said, showing his frosty white teeth. He sat down across from me.

A waiter came for our order, and I was too relieved because I was burning up: sweating like I was out in the sun. Nothing like this had ever happened to me before; this was the type of thing I only daydreamed about. My life was boring. The same page, day after day.

"I don't know what type of drink to order," I admitted, glancing nervously at him. "Why don't you order for me?"

"We'll have two Scorpions," Kwame told the thick-behind waitress who stood there blushing and smiling. She scribbled quickly on her notepad. I felt a twinge of jealousy when Kwame smiled back, and was happy as hell when the waitress switched her super-thick badonkadonk away to fill our orders. Kwame had a way with woman. He hypnotized them without saying much at all and I didn't want to share him. Tonight, I wanted all of his attention.

"What in the world is a Scorpion?" I asked, leaning on the table.

Kwame reclined in his seat and loosened the top button on his shirt, all while contemplating me. Damn. No matter what he did, Kwame was sexy.

"It has light rum, dark rum, brandy, orange and lime juice with a few other ingredients. You'll like it," he assured me.

"I'd better," I teased.

"So, Mrs. Kendra," Kwame leaned forward and cupped my hand inside his two massive ones. "While we wait for our drinks, would you like to do some karaoke?"

"Karaoke?!" I looked at the two couples awaiting their turn by the machine. "I don't think so."

"Come on. Loosen up."

"Do you see these stilettos I have on?"

I stuck one of my legs out so Kwame could get a good view of what he'd been staring at earlier.

"What are you worried about, falling?"

"That, or hitting a bad note."

"If it makes you feel any better, I can't carry a tune either, and you don't have to worry about falling. Nobody falls doing karaoke unless their drunk out of their minds. But if you do fall, I'll catch you."

Of that I had no doubt. Not even a dress shirt could hide Kwame's beefy build. I almost shivered.

"Alright," I decided.

Kwame stretched out his hand, and I allowed him to help me to my feet. He was the perfect gentleman, letting me walk ahead of him. At the karaoke machine the other two couples graciously stepped aside so we could go next. I laughed as Kwame sang an old school song: "Can We Talk," by Tevin Campbell. He wasn't a bad singer. He wasn't good, either; however, what he lacked vocally he made up for in the sexy way he moved. When my turned came, I hopped up on the platform and sang Aretha Franklin's "Jump To It."

When I was done, Kwame grasped my hand and helped me off the platform. All the ladies were ogling at him, but he was mine's for the night and I was proud to be with him. We watched the other couples take their turn. Before long we were laughing and chiming in. Kwame took my hand and we began to dance. He spun me around, pulled me close to him, wrapped his hands around my waist, then slid his hands onto my hips, where they stayed. Lord have mercy, my body was going crazy. I could not breathe as we rocked, making our own rhythm.

Kwame's body felt good—too good. I hated when the song ended. He and I clapped along with the other couples before walking back to our seats. The waitress was just replacing our drinks on the table. Ever the gentleman, Kwame pulled out my chair before taking his own seat. Removing the cloth napkin from the table, Kwame wiped the sweat from his face and smooth bald head.

I took a sip of my drink.

"How is it?" he asked.

"Oh man, this is good," I nodded my head in approval.

"See, I told you," he said, taking a sip of his own. "Are you enjoying yourself?"

"Yeah, I have to do this more often."

"Yes, you do. And I'm going to see to it that you do."

"Okay, I'm holding you to that."

I laughed as we clinked our glasses. For the first time, I fully realized all the things I'd been missing out on. The whole world was out there and I was letting it slip through my fingers like sand.

Kwame moved his drink aside and folded his hands on the table.

"So, Mrs. Kendra. What else do you like to do besides dancing?"

"Well, I like cooking and taking care of my daughter…"

"No," he laughed and enveloped my hand within his. "I mean, what else do you like to do for fun?"

"To tell you the truth, I haven't had fun in so long. I don't know what I like anymore."

"Well, I'm going to try to change that. Life is too short to let it pass you by. When you're on your deathbed, you don't want any regrets about things you didn't do, right?"

I hung my head.

"So, tell me one thing you haven't done that you want to?"

"I don't know," I shoved my shoulders up and down quickly.

"Come on," he said, covering my hand again and keeping it over mine's this time. "What is one thing you would do right now if given the opportunity."

"I guess I'd go sailing."

"Ah, sailing; you like the water?"

"Don't get me wrong," I said, swirling my straw in my drink with my free hand. "I can't swim a lick, but I love the way the sun looks when it's setting on the ocean."

"Yeah, that sounds perfect." Kwame gave me a sultry smile, removed his hand from mine and sat back in his chair, looking intently at me. "Especially if it's me and you watching the sun set together."

I blushed and hit his hand playfully.

"What about you?" I asked, taking a sip of my drink to cool me down. "What do you want to do that you haven't done already?"

"I've done almost everything I wanted to: motorcycle racing, bungee jumping, skiing…"

"Answer the question," I demanded playfully.

Kwame's eyes clouded over like I'd hit a nerve. "I guess I'd visit Ghana again."

"Well, what's stopping you? Ghana is only a plane ride away if you want to go."

Suddenly, I heard a heavy, tongue-tied voice that caught my full attention. I looked toward the bar where the voice came from, and sure enough: it was Rich's best friend Cory. Damn. I wanted to ask how his bummy ass got in here in the first place, but there he was—suit jacket complimenting his dress pants, and dreds caught up in a rubber band. I covered the side of my face with my hand and turned in the opposite direction, praying Cory hadn't seen me. The last thing I needed was for him to call Rich up and tell him I was out with another man—even if it was innocent.

"What's wrong?" Kwame's eyes narrowed in concern.

"Can we get out of here? That man over at the bar is my husband's best friend."

"Say no more," Kwame responded, holding up his hand.

I grabbed my purse quickly, keeping my back to Cory. I didn't think he saw me. Lord, I sure hoped not. Kwame steered me back into the restaurant and I let out a sigh of relief. I was ready to go home but Kwame suggested we go somewhere else.

"Where?" I questioned him. It was still early and I was having a good time.

He was about to tell me when my cell phone began blowing up.

"Yeah, Daddy," I grumbled.

"Ain't that much talking in the world, child. It's eleven at night. When you coming to get your daughter?"

"Give me an hour."

"Thirty minutes," he said with finality.

Kwame was smiling and shaking his head when I clicked the end button.

"Let me guess—Daddy Isaac?"

"What else is new," I said as we both shared a laugh. "My dad is a trip."

He walked me to my car and opened the door for me.

"Hold on, I have something for you."

Kwame ran off to his truck and returned a few minutes later with a colorful green, yellow and black quilt.

"This is for you," he held it out to me.

Damn, this man made me feel special.

"It's beautiful," I gushed. "What is it?"

"Kente cloth. It's from my country. Each color has its own symbolic meaning."

"I love it. Thank you."

We stood enjoying each other's presence for a few seconds before Kwame grasped my hand and kissed it.

"I had a lovely evening with you, Mrs. Kendra."

"So did I," I replied, not blinking or even moving away from Kwame. The only thing missing that would compete the night was a kiss. Kwame eased closer to me and I licked my lips—ready, eager, only he kissed my cheek instead. He remained close to my cheek for a few

more seconds, like he was contemplating something. I silently wished whatever he was contemplating he would go on ahead and do;
however, the only thing Kwame did was whisper
for me to have a good night. I was disappointed
but I thanked him anyway before slipping inside
my Range Rover.

"I'll see you tomorrow," Kwame told me.

"Tomorrow?" I asked excitedly.

"I have to finish planting those rosebushes for
you."

I waved at Kwame, cranked up the engine
and drove away. This was the best night I'd had
in years, and now that I'd gotten a taste of fun—
real fun—I couldn't see my ass sitting in the
house all alone, waiting on Rich, ever again.

7

Ever had one thing happen in your life that made you question every decision and action you ever made? That's what was going on with me at that moment. I was mixed up. Confused. Questioning everything about my life. Even though it was late: one in the morning, I called April and told her everything. April had told me I could call her anytime. Besides, it's not like April hasn't called me late several times herself.

"I think I married the wrong man," I whispered into the telephone when I was finished.

April yawned.

"Why would you think Rich is the wrong man? Because he doesn't spend any time with you?"

"It's more than that," I twirled the phone cord nervously. "The only thing Rich and I have in common is our daughter. When we're together it's dull as hell. I mean, do you remember how I was in school?"

"You were popular with the boys, that's for sure," April yawned again. "You even stole my boyfriend. What was his name?"

"Tony Woods, and I did not steal him from you. I was in no way attracted to him. I was just as surprised as you were when he kissed me at your seventeenth birthday party."

"Then why did you screw him?"

"I was high. They spiked the punch, remember?"

April laughed hysterically. "Anyway, was Tony good in bed?"

"He was horrible," I laughed along with her. "He didn't even know which hole to stick it in."

April and I continued to laugh over that teenage event until I put us back on topic. "Anyway, I'm trying to make a point here."

"Please hurry, we only have a few hours left before work."

"All I'm saying is: I'm home all the time. I never do anything or go anyplace. It's like I'm just waiting on Rich to make me happy but I don't think he can." I laid on my bed careful so as not to wake Bree. "What if Rich isn't the man for me?"

"This wouldn't have anything to do with Kwame, would it?"

"He just has me thinking," I let out a weary breath. "We had so much fun. It's like he's was on my level. We're compatible."

"And now you're ready to do what?"

"I think I want to divorce Rich."

"Are you serious? You run into this man—who, I might add, is the yardman—you have a few drinks and now you're questioning your marriage. How many Scorpions did you drink tonight?"

"Only one. I'm sober. It's just… I can't explain it but it's like Kwame brought me back to life. He reminded me of how I wanted to live my life. I want to have fun. Do things, go places and meet people."

"And you can't do that and stay in your marriage?"

"If I stay with Rich, I won't. All he wants to do is sit home and work and save money. We never spend. I want a man who I can enjoy my life with. Hell, I'm young. I want to live before I get old and can't do shit or look good doing it."

"I still say you need to sit Rich down and talk to him. Tell him you're not happy. Sometimes, in a marriage, it won't be 50/50. Sometimes one partner will give more than the other, but you have to do everything in your power to work out your marriage. Trust me on this: your husband is working to give you a better life and everything you want. He loves you. Really loves you. And love is better than fleeting infatuation."

"Ugh… I'm miserable," I thumped my head hard on the pillow.

"I think the Scorpion is talking," April giggled. "I had one a few weeks ago and when I woke up the next morning, my husband told me I'd made love to him in the back seat of the car."

I laughed, feeling a little better.

"Sleep it off and talk to me tomorrow, okay?"

"Oh, alright."

~~~~

I told April goodnight and hung up the telephone. I was not high. I didn't feel high, either. I was in my right mind. I threw the cover to the other side of the bed, confused now more than ever. Over the past few days I'd known Kwame, we just clicked. We were compatible. He had the same interests and he loved to have fun. He made me feel good. Rich didn't make me feel that way. Sometimes I could look at Rich and feel nothing but anger. I loved Rich, but not with a fiery hot love. It was more like the love I'd have for a brother or cousin. Not saying I'd fuck my cousin or brother if I had one, but that was the kind of love I felt for him. It wasn't that type of love that made your heart race or send chills over your flesh from just a look at the person. I felt dirty admitting that to myself. But it was the truth. I didn't know when or how it happened, but my love for Rich was not the same anymore.

I fell into a restless sleep an hour later.

8

My alarm clock didn't go off the next morning. I didn't wake up until eight thirty.

"Daddy, why didn't you wake me up at seven?!" I complained while I rushed around the house getting myself and Bree ready.

"You're grown," he snapped, face set in a hard, grim line as he sat back in his recliner watching "Good Morning America." "And that's what you get staying out half the night instead of coming in at a decent hour."

Daddy Isaac sat up in his cushioned chair long enough to smirk at me.

"Call your husband 'cause I ain't no answering service. He called about ten times last night."

I wanted to scream. Daddy really pushed me to the edge sometimes. I finished dressing and left, slamming the door behind me and Bree.

I ended up staying at Bree's school for twenty minutes because she had a bad temper tantrum. By the time I made it to school, it was almost nine thirty. April was overloaded when I walked in the classroom. Bad day already. One of the students had thrown up all over the floor and two others were fighting. April cut her eyes at me.

She always wanted things perfect, especially her classroom, and I had thrown things off. To make up for it I bought April lunch later that day.

~~~~

By the time I left school, I was exhausted. The minute I got in my car I pulled my heels off and put on my flip-flops. Thankfully, I still had a couple of hours before I had to pick Bree up. When I got home Daddy Isaac's Cadillac was gone: he had an appointment with the doctor that afternoon. Kwame was out in the yard, sweating and finishing up the rosebushes. He stood even before I made it over to him. Our gazes met for a long, passionate moment before Kwame slowly looked me up and down. I felt beautiful—like I was something of value. I hadn't been looked at that way in a long time, and I must admit: it felt good. I stepped in front of Kwame, looking up at him because he was so tall.

"Last night was fun," I said, touching his arm.

"We will do it again," Kwame's deep African tenor rumbled in response. He dug his shovel into the ground, looking at me with that super-glue stare again. I forced my gaze onto the rosebuses Kwame had planted near the side windows and gathered my senses.

"So, how do you like them?" he asked.

"They look pretty," I voiced my approval, looking at Kwame again.

"Yes, they do," he agreed, eyes still on me.

I couldn't help but think Kwame was saying that about me instead of the flowers.

"I'm planting the last one now," he informed me.

"Hey, why don't I get you a glass of water," I offered, noticing the sweat tickling down his face. I couldn't lie: I wanted to lick him dry. "I'll change clothes and help you plant that last rosebush, too," I added, walking away.

"No, Kendra," he stopped me, pulling off his work gloves. "A pretty lady like you should not be in the dirt. And what about your legs—the ant bites?"

"Didn't I dance with you last night?" I turned and smiled. "My legs are fine."

I dashed into the house. Upstairs in my bed-room I slipped into my skinny jeans and a tank top, listening to the messages on the answering machine as I dressed. Rich's croaky voice came through.

"Hey, it's me. Couldn't reach you yesterday. How was school for you and Bree? Call me when you get in."

Beep! Message two.

"Kendra, where are you? I know school is out. Give me a call."

Beep! Message three.

"If you're home, pick up. We need to talk."

Beep! Message four.

"Stop being so childish, Kendra. We are both adults here. Pick up the damned phone and talk to me."

Beep. End of messages.

My lips curled in glee. Now Rich knew how it felt to be ignored. I ain't gonna lie: it felt good for the shoe to be on the other foot.

~~~~

I checked myself in the mirror. I looked good and the jeans made my butt look big. Satisfied, I went back outside. Kwame had laid a towel down on the ground for me.

"I wouldn't want you to bruise your knees," he said.

I wanted to laugh. Kwame was too good to me: he made me feel like a lady. Rich could take a few tips from him.

I knelt beside Kwame. He moved in closer until we were shoulder to shoulder. Arm to arm. Faces so close we could almost touch cheeks. He handed me some work gloves. The rosebush was already in the hole Kwame had prepared for it. Together he and I began covering it with organic soil and soil conditioner.

"I bet your yard is beautiful," I said, smoothing out the soil.

"I don't have a yard. I stay in a condo downtown. But I do have a lot of plants in my home to remind me of Ghana."

Kwame took off his work gloves, pulled a pair of garden scissors from his pocket, cut a rose from the bush and gently placed it under my nose. I closed my eyes, inhaling the intoxicating fragrance. Deftly removing all of the thorns, Kwame tucked the rose behind my ear, all while keeping his gaze on me.

"You are very beautiful," he whispered.

My heart leaped from my chest and my cheeks began to burn. We returned to patting the soil. By mistake our hands collided—his on top of mines, mines on top of his, then entwined. Slowly, I looked up, only to catch his dreamy gaze already on me. The electricity I'd felt yesterday took over and my clitoris began pounding like my heart. I blinked, trying to find enough self-control to walk away—run—but my mind turned to mush and my body took on a mind of its own. The next thing I knew, my lips were brushing against Kwame's, and I was pulling his bottom lip between mine's. Then he was pulling my top lip between his. Kwame was the perfect kisser. Our tongues met, and we began exploring each other's mouths. His swiftly flickering tongue beat mine into submission.

The poor soil was left unattended while the scent of roses surrounded us, pulling us deeper into one another. A moan escaped my throat.

Kwame tasted sweet; smelled so good I forgot I was in my front yard—in my neighborhood where I'd been raised and everyone knew me. I felt like I was dreaming again. This couldn't be real. I wanted it to be, but this was all in my head. My fantasy. My mind playing tricks on me. I heard a horn bomp, snatching me back to reality. Wiping my mouth, I jerked away from Kwame. It was real. What was I thinking? My next door neighbor could have been peeping from her shades, like she usually does. Thank God no one was, and thank God the car bomping was down the street and no one was outside. Kwame was still staring at me, looking hungry—desperate. He wanted me just as much as I wanted him. I couldn't take anymore.

"Let me…let me get your water," I stuttered nervously.

Jumping up, I rushed into the house and headed straight for the kitchen. I ran cool water in the sink, splashing some of it over my face before patting myself dry with a paper towel. All of my strength was gone. I was weak, spent, and my heart refused to slow down although I struggled to make sense of what just happened. I heard the front door open and close. Oh Lord, don't let it be him, I prayed. The footsteps were coming closer and closer. My heart was thundering in my ears. I was too fragile. Too dizzy. Too aroused. Too deep into temptation. I wanted Kwame. I needed him. My body was screaming for him—this man I hardly knew—yet felt a strong sexual connection to.

I felt Kwame near me. His eyes burned holes through my back, making me shudder. I grabbed a glass from the opened dishwasher and removed the ice tray from the freezer.

"Kendra," he stopped behind me. "I'm so sorry. I got carried away."

My brain was spinning as I loosened the ice. What did he mean he got carried away? I wanted Kwame to get carried away—to make love until my body convulsed with orgasm after orgasm—until I could speak no more. Think no more. Until the ache between my legs subsided.

"I'll leave if you want," he whispered, so close I could feel his breath hot on my neck. The glass filled with ice fell from my shaking hands into the sink, shattering. I turned to face Kwame, pressing my hands on the counter behind me for support.

"Do you want me to leave?" he asked, his voice barely audible.

His sexy eyes narrowed and his dimples deepened as he licked his lips. I swore I could see his heart pounding through his heaving chest. I was burning up inside. Kwame pressed into me until there was no space to move. The pressure from the enormous wedge on the center of my jeans caused my clitoris to go into spasms. I lowered my head, feeling weaker than I'd ever felt. My heart was thrashing, my hands shaking, my body wet—sizzling. This is what Eve must have felt in the Garden of Eden, I thought. This wicked temptation. This snake offering fruit that was forbidden.

"I take your silence as yes. I'll go."

Kwame backed off and turned away. Without thinking, I reached for his wrist.

"No, don't," I begged him.

Before the next words spilled out, he snatched me into himself. We began kissing so hard it looked like we were attacking each other. His hands on my breast, my hands on his back—his ass. His hand on my private area, fondling it right through the jeans. I reached for the knot in Kwame's pants, caressing it gently. He heaved great big gulps of air as he unbuckled his belt and tugged down his jeans. I stepped out of my flip-flops and Kwame slipped me out of my skinny jeans so smoothly you would have thought I had oil slicked on my body.

He whipped out his penis.

Hard.

Big.

Unbelievably big.

I wanted it—him—but at the same time, I was scared in an excited kind of way. Kwame began stroking his penis with his hand. He spun me around. Bent me over: face down, ass up. Damn near ripped me out of my panties. Parted my legs wider than Moses parted The Red Sea. Slowly, he filled me with every delicious inch of his hard on. I screamed out in contentment, my body already accepting him.

Kwame buried his face in the crook of my neck, letting me adjust to his size. Then he began rocking hard. Strong. To a supernatural rhythm that rendered me astonished. Both hands pressed into my shoulders then cupped my breasts before resting on my hips, guiding my movements. I gripped the counter and tried to speak but sounded like I was speaking in a foreign language. So much pleasure was shooting through my body I felt insane. Kwame knew my hot spots. His tongue delved into my ear. He licked my neck, fingered my clit, pinched my nipples, all while slamming in deep—hitting home. My eyes welled with tears. Nothing had ever felt this good. Ever. A super strong orgasm slammed over me. My legs gave out, but Kwame held me up, still going and going like that damned bunny on TV.

A few minutes later, Kwame's breathing picked up—then he was gasping. He was ready to release, so like the rapper Juvenile said: I backed that ass up, helping him out. He circled his arms around my waist, did a few shallow thrust, massaged my g-spot, then slammed into me one final time, grinding and trembling. I came again. I couldn't see Kwame's facial expressions, but if they were anything like his moans, I surmised he was just as pleased as I was.

Weak, Kwame lost his balance and fell to the floor with me right behind him.

Spent, out of breath, we both still managed to laugh.

"I thought you said you'd catch me if I fell."

"That was last night, when I had all of my strength. I'm too drained, woman."

Kwame drew me into his arms. He kissed my neck, my back, smacked my ass; his sweat mingling with mine's as we both tried to recover. Then Kwame ran his hand through my hair and buried his face in it, kissing it.

"You are beautiful—amazing," he said, finding his voice.

Boy, did I feel that way; and I was satisfied: the pounding between my legs was testimony to how good Kwame had pleased me. He kissed me on the side of my face then planted a slow, lazy kiss on my lips. Kwame was the one who was amazing, I thought. He worked my body like he'd been privy to my dreams—fantasies—and knew just want I wanted and needed done.

Extending his hand, Kwame helped me up and began fixing his clothes.

~~~~

"I want to see you again," he told me.

"When?"

"Tomorrow. Thirty-eighth and Lennox at five."

He kissed me again and left just in time: Daddy Isaac's car pulled into the driveway not five minutes later. I fixed up my clothes, cleaned up the shattered glass, and dashed upstairs to the room right before my dad walked into the house. I worried that he would notice something was off. But then he shouted:

"Kendra, why you left the damned dishwasher open?! And the knives are sticking straight up on the sharp side?! You trying to kill me?"

I let out a sigh of relief, glad he hadn't noticed a thing.

9

Rich

Since the day Kendra and I tied the knot, she's been complaining. About stupid shit, too. Ain't nothing worse than a nagging woman. Worse than a fly buzzing in your ear.

Kendra loves saying I never do nothing with her or for her. Sometimes I wondered why she wanted me around. What does she need me for? Maybe she likes fussing and fighting with me. That's about all she does, too. Complain and talk trash. Sometimes she even calls me names. She thinks she'll find better but there ain't too many men out there who would put up with her bullshit or treat her the way I do. Any other man would have been done hightailed it out of here a long time ago, but I stayed around because I loved her. Couldn't see myself without her. And besides, we got a daughter together, and I ain't letting no other man raise my seed.

My mama left my biological father when I was a baby and married my stepfather when I was three, and he would beat my ass for no reason at all. And don't even let me get started on the mental abuse I endured from that fool. From the time I was six 'til I was about fourteen, he was always telling me I ain't shit, and constantly throwing me out on the streets. My grandmother finally got tired of it and took me in. So I know no man will treat or love my daughter the same way I do. Divorcing Kendra and losing my daughter is not an option. I made up my mind when I married her she would be the woman I stayed with for the rest of my life. Nothing she does, has done or can do will run me off. Nothing. I am determined to keep my family together.

I do love Kendra—with everything within me. I would die for her in the blink of an eye. That's how strong my love is for her. I may not show it the way she wants me to, but since when is taking a woman out or buying her presents or opening car doors or putting a coat down over a puddle so she can walk over it or complementing her or pulling out chairs the only way to show a woman love? That's superficial shit; it don't amount to a hill of beans. True love is staying with a woman through thick and thin. Sickness and health; rich and poor. I show my love by working, by taking care of her and my daughter when they're sick. Man, I even took care of her father after we got married. He was so sick he couldn't get out of bed. I would change his bedpans, feed him. And why? Because I loved her. But Kendra wants a fantasy. A man who will give her all the attention she craves, entertain her, hold down a full time job, and make love to her for hours at a time.

Unrealistic.

Most of the time I'm so tired when I get home, I can hardly make love for five minutes; and if Kendra's riding me—three. When we first got together I knew we were opposite as night and day. I was a homebody; content with a movie and dinner. On the other hand, Kendra got bored too quickly and always wanted to try something new. She would change her mind like she changed her clothes. Unpredictable; restless, moody and bitching all the time. Like most men, I have a short fuse. But I ignored her and looked past all of her aggravating ways. I told myself she would change. Her looks along with her bomb sex blinded me.

I flipped through the channels on the motel television. The place I was staying in is clean: with cable, free high speed internet access, a pool, and even a spa downstairs—where most of the men who traveled out of town with me are. Some locals from a beauty pageant are staying in the same motel with us, frolicking around in damned near nothing. A few of my friends knocked on my door twenty minutes ago and asked me to join them. Told me to come downstairs. Said the women were all dimes. I declined. My mind was, and still is, on Kendra. Man this love thing is strange. An enigma. It'll have you doing crazy shit like calling a woman back to back.

I done called Kendra fifteen times today and she ain't answer. If she knew why I'd been working so hard for the past year she wouldn't have treated me the way she been. I feel my heart in my stomach whenever I think about the surprise I have in store for her when I return home Monday. Then she'll see why I been working so hard, and why I'm so damned tired most of the time. She thinks I spend my Sundays off hanging with Cory, but for the past six months I've been getting together the biggest surprise of her life. I know she'll be happy when I reveal it. She'll probably never give me a hard time again.

I sat down on my bed thinking about how childish Kendra was being. Her daddy got her that way. Spoiled her rotten from the day she was born and still treats her like a baby. Kendra is a twenty-four-year-old spoiled brat. "Cute brat," I mumbled, smiling to myself. And I know she ain't never leaving Daddy Isaac until they put him in the ground. Shoot, I love her daddy like he's my daddy. He's like the father I never had.

A knock on the motel door interrupted me. The door opened a cracked and Rudolph, one of the men who traveled out of town with me, entered the room. He was hugged up on a voluptuous Hispanic woman dressed in a thong and bra top bikini.

"Hey, man, you missing out on all the action. The party's downstairs."

"Nah, I'm good," I said, waving him away. I sat up and scooted to the edge of the bed. "I gotta call Kendra."

Rudolph sucked his teeth and flipped his hand at me in contempt.

"Man, Kendra got you whupped," he said, closing the door behind him.

I shook my head. Rudolph's married—been married for eight years and has a five kids. Every time we go out of town, he cheats. A lot of men who work with me cheat—because they can. 'What the wife don't know, won't hurt her' is their motto. But I don't believe that, because I wouldn't want Kendra doing anything behind my back. So I'm faithful. And it's not because I can't get a woman. I done had plenty of women throwing it at me. Pretty women, too. But I ain't never cheated on Kendra and never will. No woman is worth losing her over. I don't give a damn if she's got an ass made out of platinum. I ain't doing nothing to risk my family.

I speed-dialed Kendra again. It was five in the evening. She had to be home. I didn't know why she's acting like this.

"Hello?"

It was Kendra's dad.

"Hey, Pops. Where in the world is Kendra? She wouldn't answer my calls yesterday or the day before that."

"She's gone. Said she got a school meeting."

"Again?"

"That's what I asked her."

"Did she take Bree?" I asked, resting my back on a king-sized pillow.

"Nope, I got her right here in the chair beside me."

"Well, how is Bree?" I asked next, smiling at the thought of her.

"She's alright. We was dozing off 'fore you woke us up."

"I'll let y'all get back to sleep then."

"Hold up, wait a minute. When you coming home, boy?"

"Next Monday, Pops."

I remembered the surprise I had planned for Kendra and can't keep it in anymore.

"Hey look, I'm gonna tell you something and I don't want you to tell Kendra."

"Go on."

"I got a big surprise for her. You know how for the past six months I've been working all the time?"

"Son, I ain't got all evening, just tell me."

"I brought Kendra a daycare!"

"You what?"

"You know how she's been saying she wanted to start a daycare for autistic children? Well, I brought her a daycare building on Eighty-third."

"Go on, son! That's alright," Daddy Isaac said laughing.

"So, I'm coming home Monday and I'ma surprise her with it. Please don't tell her, Pops."

"I ain't gonna say a thing. You alright, son. I'm glad you my son-in-law."

I laughed when I heard him laughing again.

"Make sure you tell Kendra to call me, okay?"

"I will," he chuckled.

After ending the call I lay back on the bed with my arms spread out behind my head, trying to picture the look on Kendra's face when she sees her new daycare center Monday.

10

Kendra

"Are you serious?"

I looked at Kwame in complete shock.

"You taking me sailing?"

He caressed my cheek gently and said, "It's what you said you'd do if you had a chance. I'm going to make that happen."

Every thought escaped my brain when Kwame took my hand and led me onto the boat. The man was something special. Damn, why hadn't I met him before Rich? Why was life so unfair? Why couldn't I turn back the hands of time? Or reverse the Earth?

"The boat is mine for the rest of the night," Kwame said, guiding me inside for a short tour.

It was incredible. Flat screen television. Comfortable setting area. And plenty of drinks.

"Let me introduce you to the Captain." Kwame steered me in the direction of a tall gentleman with a full beard who was dressed in a crisp white uniform. The captain shook my hand firmly.

"A meal is being prepared for you all on the deck," he informed us. "It should be ready shortly."

I felt like I was in an exotic dream. This was how I had imagined my life would be when I was back in high school.

Kwame led me to a room on the boat that had a bed. As he took off my clothes, I made myself concentrate on only him. There was no Rich, no Daddy, and no boring life along with its disappointments. There was just Kwame's body all over my body. I stared at his face for a while before my gaze slid below to his penis. The way Kwame had ruled me with it yesterday made me instantly wet.

"I haven't been able to think about anything except you since yesterday," he whispered in his erotic accent.

"Me neither," I sighed, licking his lips.

"I missed you," Kwame moaned.

He smothered me with kisses. In no time we were rolling on the bed. I don't know what took over my body: maybe it was the fact that I'd been dick deprived for so long. When I got on his erection, I clamped on it tighter than a shell over a pearl. Kwame whispered obscenities, bobbing his head from side to side like he was possessed. I began moving my hips like I had no bones. Kwame grabbed those hips, moving with me.

Up and down.

In and out.

Around and around.

We were one.

Perfect.

Minutes later, we came together. Shook together. Moaned together. And collapsed against each other trying to catch our breath. After we rested, he and I were both greedy for more. We did it again and again and again. Kwame was an animal! When we were finally done, I watched to see if he would fall asleep like Rich usually did; but to my surprise, Kwame didn't. He stood and told me he was checking on dinner. I smiled. For once I didn't have to worry about a man ignoring me and falling asleep after sex. This time it was me who took a nap.

~~~~

Dinner was waiting when Kwame woke me half an hour later. I was starving and ready to eat, but I couldn't find my underwear. I tore the room up—practically had everything upside down—but nothing. I decided to just take a shower and join Kwame. The ocean was beautiful: the sun setting, along with its reflection on the water, was perfect. The chef had prepared a perfect Ghanaian meal of chicken stew, Jollof Rice, Fufu, boiled yams, eggplant and Gari biscuits. I was so stuffed, I could not move. I sipped my drink and focused on getting to know even more about Kwame.

"So tell me why you don't have a wife, Kwame?" I asked, pushing my drink aside.

"Because you're already taken," he shot back.

I waved my hand at him.

"I'm serious," I said.

Kwame wiped his mouth.

"I just got out of a relationship," he confessed.

"What happened?"

"She moved away."

"Did you love her?"

"No; do you love your husband?"

The question threw me for a loop.

"Why would you ask me that?" I wanted to know.

"You're here with me, aren't you? So, there obviously is an issue."

"Let's just say I'm not happy," I stated plainly, taking another sip of my drink.

"Neither was I." Kwame leaned forward and peered at me. "Life is too short to waste it with someone you're not happy with."

His hypnotic eyes held me even after he'd said that.

"Come here," Kwame said seductively. I walked around the table and he pulled me on his lap. "I want to make you happy."

The kiss he gave me made me want to do it to him again. When I finished slobbing him down, I took off my necklace and placed it around his neck.

"What's this?"

"The only thing I have from my mother."

"And you're giving it to me?"

"Yeah." I kissed him again. "Today I've been happier than I've been in my entire life."

If my cell phone hadn't gone off, I probably would have sat there watching Kwame watch me for the rest of the night. I got up from Kwame's lap. He arose from the table, wrapped his arms around me and sucked on my neck.

"Your husband?"

I nodded. Kwame kissed me on the forehead.

"Think about what I told you. You deserve to be happy, Kendra."

I let out a long sigh, and watched him walk away. I decided to let Rich go to voice mail once again. I could see land. The boat would be docking soon. One thing was for sure: Kwame had rocked my world.

I had some serious thinking to do.

~~~~

The next few days, Kwame and I had so much fun, I hated to go home. Daddy kept Bree because he thought I was attending afterschool meetings.

Kwame and I went to the movies and to a club out of town where no one knew us. We danced and partied until the wee hours of the morning. We didn't hang out much in town because I was scared we would run into one of Rich's friends, like that time we bumped into Cory at Passion's Restaurant.

Kwame's house ended up being the perfect getaway. The man cooked and wined and dined me; and when we made love afterwards, the man brought me to powerful orgasms that put me to sleep.

He also knew how to hold a solid conversation about something other than his boring job or sports.

Kwame was the entire package. And I couldn't lie to myself: I was already in love with him.

11

April must have stared at me for a good minute before she said anything.

"You slept with Kwame? But what about Rich? What about your family?"

I looked at the students running and playing on the playground.

"April, I told you before: things were not peaches and cream between us. I was lonely. Kwame...damn... he made me feel like a woman again."

"But what about your marriage?"

"What about it?" I put my head down, feeling defeated. "I'm not happy. Life is too short not to be happy," I said, repeating the words Kwame had told me.

"Oh, Kendra. You can't seriously be thinking of ending your marriage over Kwame?"

"It's not because of Kwame. It's because of Rich. You'll never understand how it feels when your husband takes you for granted. Never. I don't want to go back to the life I have with Rich. Being ignored. Never going anyplace. Never being complimented."

"I wish I had never referred him to you," April shook her head.

"Girl, please. It's not your fault I cheated on Rich."

"You weren't thinking about this until you met Kwame," April sneered. "I'm going to be honest: I think Rich is a good man and I really like him. That man loves you. He's working hard so the two of you can have a better life. You don't even know Kwame. You're just infatuated with him. You can't seriously be thinking about risking your marriage over a man you've known for a month. So what are you going to do, Kendra?"

"I'm gonna separate from Rich," I decided that very moment.

~~~

The instant I walked through the door, the smell of oregano and bay leaves hit me.

"Daddy!" I called from the hallway. "What you cooking?"

Rich stepped out into the hallway with two glasses filled with what looked like wine.

"I love it when you call me Daddy," he joked.

I felt like I'd stepped into the twilight zone. There was no way my husband was in an apron, handing me a glass of wine and cooking.

"What are you doing home?" I wondered.

"We finished up earlier than I thought."

Suddenly I lost the nerve to tell Rich what I'd been practicing the entire ride home.

"What's going on?" I asked instead.

"I'm spending the evening with my wife, that's what's going on."

"Where's my dad? Bree?"

"At your aunt's place for the evening."

"Are you alright? What's gotten into you?'

Rich laughed and took my purse.

"Woman, you are a trip. First you beg me to spend time and do things with you, and then when I do, you still complain. Just come sit your fine ass down."

I sat at the table, numb, as Rich served me the dinner he cooked while steadily showering me with kisses.

"Eat up, baby," he instructed. "After dinner I have something special for you."

12

Life is a trip. All I know is: the moment I stopped caring about Rich and spread my thighs to another man, and gave what was supposed to be sacred between husband and wife away, Rich begin changing right before my eyes.

"What's this key for?" I asked.

We were downtown in a big building on the second floor.

"Behind those double doors will explain why I've been absent so much," Rich replied.

I really didn't feel well. The Italian feast Rich cooked for dinner traveled from my stomach back up my throat as I unlock the doors. Inside, it looked like a school. There were tables and toys and classrooms and a huge office.

"This is your new daycare, baby."

And then it all registered. Hand held over my mouth, I rushed from room to room. Finally, I found the bathroom and turned on the water, dashing it all over my face. My knees buckled before finally giving out.

~~~~

"Baby, you okay?" Rich hurried to my side. He grabbed a towel, wiped my face then helped me from the floor.

"I guess I got excited," I panted, swallowing the vomit that wanted to come out.

"How do you feel?"

"I'm fine now."

I washed my hands, and then Rich held me by my waist from behind as we went from room to room.

"This is why I was working so hard, Kendra."

Tears came to my eyes.

"I wanted to spend time with you, but I also wanted to make your dreams come true. I love you with all of this," Rich thumped his chest. "I hope you'll forget about all our fights."

I was too baffled to think straight.

"Why didn't you tell me?" I wailed, trying to control my emotions. "You should have told me."

"There was no guarantee I would get this place, Kendra. I didn't want to get your hopes up and disappoint you, so I kept it to myself. When I finally signed the lease I waited because I wanted to surprise you today."

"What are you talking about?"

"Today is our six year anniversary."

I felt lower than whale shit. How could I forget the day I got married? Not only did I feel guilty, I was also angry. If he had just told me, I wouldn't have fucked another man. Maybe I wouldn't have been so hard on him, or fallen out of love with him.

"You forgot. I knew you did when you didn't say anything at dinner."

I was about to apologize when Rich muted me.

"I can't blame you. I got a lot of making up to do. I have another surprise. Tonight we're not going home; your bags are already packed and in the truck."

~~~~~

We ended up at the beach. Rich knew I loved the beach. Always have. But this was the first time I hated it. We had a fabulous room near the ocean, and ate dinner at a great spot on the strip. That night we made love. No, we really had good sex! I was surprised because Rich took his time and made sure I got off twice. I mean, I didn't think I would come with all the guilt swimming around inside my head, but Rich did things I didn't even know he could do. He licked places I had never paid attention to. He touched places that made me cream. Afterwards, Rich didn't go to sleep: he hugged me and kissed me and told me he loved me more than life itself.

"I'm sorry I always fall asleep on you after we make love," Rich apologized. "It's just that I be so tired from working all the time."

I felt so stupid and guilty. I couldn't even look Rich in the eyes. Instead, I focused on his forehead the entire weekend.

13

As soon as I got home, I called Kwame. Rich had taken the car to the car wash so I had the house to myself.

"Kendra, where have you been? I missed—"

"I can't see you anymore, Kwame," I blurted out.

"What are you saying? What are you talking about?"

"We were a mistake. What I did was a mistake."

I could hear Kwame breathing hard into the phone.

"Where is this coming from?" he finally asked.

"I'm working things out with my husband."

"Where are you?"

"Home. Why?

"I want to talk to you."

"There is nothing to talk about."

"We have a lot to talk about. You can't just cut me off…Can I come over?"

"No. Hell, nah. Rich will be back any minute."

"Then meet me."

"I can't," I snapped, suddenly stressed the hell out.

Rich's truck pulled up in the driveway.

"I gotta go," I told Kwame. "Forget about us, okay?"

I snapped my cell phone shut. Feeling uneasy, I walked to the door to meet my husband. I had a lot of making up to do.

~~~~

The next day at school, while the kids were outside during recess, I updated April on everything that had happened recently. I told her how I'd ended things with Kwame and how Rich had brought me a daycare center.

"He told me about the daycare," April revealed.

"What? Why didn't you tell me?"

"Because he made me promise I wouldn't. Why do you think I kept trying to stand up for Rich?"

My eyes twitched.

"April, that was dumb as hell." I swallowed the other curse words I wanted to spit at her. "You so wrong for that. You dead wrong for not telling me."

April looked miserable. "How am I wrong?"

"All I'm saying is: I would have told you. Especially if I knew you was going through issues with your man and that would stop you from stepping out on him."

"For goodness sakes, I didn't think you would step outside of your marriage. I didn't think you would have an affair with Kwame."

I held up my hand. "Just forget about it," I muttered.

"So this is my fault?" April's face crumpled. "Please don't be mad at me."

Tears sprang from her eyes.

Too mad to remain near her dumb ass, I walked away and tended to a student instead.

14

The next week Kwame kept calling me repeatedly. I looked at the messages. Over sixty. But I avoided him, focusing on Rich, Bree and Daddy. Slowly, I started to move forward and tried to be a better wife. Although I didn't tell Rich I had an affair, I felt like I could pick up the pieces and make things right with him.

For the time being, Rich was almost always home—he wasn't putting in overtime anymore—and we began to talk. Really talk. It had been a minute since I'd just listened to him. I felt like I was getting to know him all over again and what I realized was: Rich was a really good guy. He had a good heart, and integrity, which was more than I could say about myself. My body was still craving Kwame's—no matter how hard I tried to fight it. The calls continued day in and day out. But as bad as I wanted to, I didn't answer. Then, one night, I could have sworn I saw Kwame's truck roll by my house real slow.

The next day, after school was out, I was tempted to stop by his apartment and be with him. I wanted to feel him inside my body so bad I couldn't think straight. Kwame was crack and I was a full blown crack head. But I fought the urge and went to my new daycare. Soon I'd have to put in my resignation at Creekside. I had employees to hire, but the licensing was going smoothly and I was almost ready to start enrolling kids. My womanhood was still throbbing with an ache only Kwame could stop, however. I hated that I had betrayed Rich, he was so damned good to me, but I would lay in the bed and make love to Rich and see Kwame in my mind's eye. It was him, not Rich I was fucking. I couldn't share my thoughts and desires with anyone. I was still mad at April, Daddy would have killed my ass, and I was never telling Rich. So I carried everything inside and suffered.

~~~~

A few days later when I walked through the door, no one was home. It was Friday. Daddy was at his sister's house and Rich wouldn't be home until later that evening. I didn't have to pick Bree up for a while. Later on that night I was supposed to be going to the beach with Rich and Bree, but right now I just wanted to sit on my butt because I was so exhausted from work and getting my daycare together. Actually, I wanted to go upstairs and go to sleep, but I had to pack and I had to cook a few meals so Daddy wouldn't have to while we were gone this week-end. The minute I kicked off my shoes, there was a knock on the door. I opened it and almost lost my bearings.

"Kwame … what are you…"

"Are you alone?" he whispered.

"Yes, but—"

Before I could finish, Kwame stepped in, closed the door, and looked around nervously.

"Kendra... we need to talk."

"No, I don't think so. It's over... what we had...what we did..."

His chest was heaving as he grabbed my arms gently, pressing his fingers into my biceps.

"There are some things I need to tell you," Kwame begged. "Please."

Kwame's hands on my bare arms completely weakened me. There was no time for talking. I lost all control. I leaned in and kissed him.

"Kendra, please.... No. Listen to me!" Kwame pulled away, panting and already sweating. "I have something to tell you. When we first got together I didn't know I was going to fall in love with you. I didn't know you would be so special."

Silencing Kwame, I brought my lips to his and tried to suck the juice from them.

I didn't want to hear him. I just wanted to be with him.

Heated like animals we tore off each other's clothes.

I couldn't get his meat in me fast enough.

I hiked up my skirt while Kwame yanked off my shirt, popping all of the buttons. His manhood was harder than I ever remembered. I pushed him onto the couch and jumped on top, shaking while his hardness slid inside of me. My head was set on nothing but releasing the pressure that had built up inside of me for far too long.

"I'm ready…I'm ready…I'm about to come…Oh, shit, it feels sooo good!"

I shouted the last part as my release happened. Jerking, I rested on Kwame's sweaty chest and enjoyed his final pumps, listening as he whimpered and shivered beneath me. I could feel his seed releasing, filling me up.

Click.

As soon as I heard the sound, my eyes flew to the door. In walked my dad. My heart literally stopped beating and everything appeared to be moving in slow motion. The three of us stared at each other in shock. I jumped up, pulled down my skirt and tried to find my shirt. Kwame began searching frantically for his.

"What in the hell is going on in here!" my dad shouted.

"Daddy," I said nervously. "It's not what you think."

"Not what I think? I know what the hell I see! You up in here screwing another man. Boy, you have one second to get the hell out of my house!"

Kwame looked at me. "Kendra…I'm sorry. I love you. I just want you to know I love you."

"If you don't get your ass out of here!" Daddy shouted. "I swear I'm calling the police!"

Kwame looked at me again then bolted out the door. The eyes my dad directed back at me burned with rage.

"I can't believe you in here cheating on your husband."

He was shaking so bad, it looked like even his false teeth were rattling. "I swear, if it wasn't for Rich and my granddaughter, I would put your ass out!"

"We weren't doing anything!" I insisted.

"You're a liar, Kendra! You just like your damned mama!"

"My mama?"

"Yeah. She was a tramp and so are you."

"How can you call me... Mama... that? You were the one cheating on her. You are the reason she left and got hooked on drugs."

"No, your mother left because she was screwing my brother."

His words felt like a kick to my gut.

"Liar!" I pointed a finger at him.

"I got no reason to lie. Your mama was sleeping with my brother. It had been going down for years. I didn't know shit until I came home early from work and caught them together in my bed. I made her leave. She wanted to take you but I wouldn't let her. I fought her. She cursed me out and told me I wasn't your daddy."

"What are you saying?" I shouted, tears streaming down my face. "Are you saying that Uncle Raymond is my daddy?"

"I never took the test. It hurt too much. I didn't want to know."

"Are you trying to hurt me because you're mad?"

"It's the truth, Kendra," spit flew from Daddy's mouth as he yelled. "Why do you think I never liked Raymond or wanted you around him?" He wiped tears from his face. "Still, I expected better… more from you. And now you up in here cheating on your husband." My dad put his hand to his head like he had a terrible headache. "You broke my fucking heart."

Daddy turned his back. I cried out for him but he stumbled out the door.

~~~

I waited for Daddy to come home, but he didn't. I couldn't wrap my mind around the things he'd said to me. I was so hurt and lost, I didn't know what to do. Rich made it home a few hours later. We packed up and headed to the beach for the weekend.

15

Daddy Isaac

I hadn't had a drink since the doctor told me my life depended on it, but now I wanted one so bad I was shaking like I was going through withdrawal. Withdrawal is a terrible thing and the effects it had on my body years ago when I stopped sipping were awful. But nothing was worse than the mental withdrawal. Physical withdrawal was a piece of cake compared to that. The mental part was a struggle day in and day out.

I'd started drinking in my teens and didn't stop until a few years ago when I was sixty. By then, the damage that liquor had done to my life couldn't be undone. The doctor told me my liver was in bad shape and hanging on by a string. Alcohol had always been my escape back in the day. One more sip was sure to put me six feet under, though. So, no matter how bad I wanted to sip or go to the old corners I used to hang at, I pulled my Cadillac into the driveway and eased it into the garage.

No other cars were in sight, and I was glad Kendra was already gone. I didn't want to look at her. I didn't even want to hear her voice. Seeing Kendra with that no good yardman hurt me more than the day I found her mama upstairs in bed with my brother. I just didn't understand why she would do such a thing. What the hell do women want—a no good bum who beats they ass and fills them up with babies they can't take care of? Rich was good to Kendra. He treated her and his daughter like gold. He didn't deserve any of this and I didn't know how I could look him in his face after seeing such a thing. I was beginning to think Kendra's behavior was because of me. Maybe if I hadn't spoiled her when she was little she would have been a more respectable woman. But when her mother left I felt so responsible. I had given the child all she wanted. Now she was rotten.

I thought about getting that liquor again. I saw myself twisting the cap off and taking a sip. I remembered how good it felt. Like hot coals in my cheeks. I thought about how good it felt to sip my sorrows away. I wished I still had my old friends to drink with, but most of them had died from some sort of illness associated with drinking. I refused to think on that at the time, or to let my life end like that. Hell, I had too much living to do and a granddaughter who needed me. I didn't want to leave Kendra yet. Even though I knew Rich would take good care of her, I still had to watch out for her. She was too silly and immature. Had always been like that. The girl always needed attention. I tried to tell her to listen with her eyes and not her ears. I told her a man can tell you anything, but it was what that man did that mattered. But Kendra had a hard-assed head, just like her deceased momma.

I stuck the key in the lock and turned it. I kicked off my shoes. I was tired, more mentally than anything. When I turned around, the first thing I noticed was the place was a mess. What the hell? Before I had time to think, I heard movement in the living room.

"Rich? Kendra?" I called out.

I thought for sure everyone was gone. I headed for the living room.

"They're not here," a hateful voice replied.

I damned near had a heart attack when the person came into view.

"How'd you get in here? Why are you in here? Did you tear my house up like this?"

"Never mind that, old man," the voice answered, more hateful this time.

Before I could move I saw a gun aimed right in my direction. Panic overtook me.

"Move it, old man," the voice ordered.

I did as I was told.

"Where we going?"

"For a ride in your Cadillac."

"What are you gonna do to me?"

"You're gonna have a few drinks."

"Drinks? I don't drink anymore. I can't."

The barrel of the gun pressed into my back.

"You will today."

All I could think of was Kendra as I was shoved into the garage. She was in deep trouble and didn't even know it. Sad thing was: I would never be able to warn her.

16

Kendra

When we arrived home Sunday the first thing I saw was a cup and a big empty liquor bottle on the table. My heart stopped.

"Daddy!" I screamed.

I ran from room to room, praying the entire time. Had what I done caused him to drink a whole bottle of liquor? When I got to Daddy Isaac's room, I noticed his bed was neatly made. Daddy never made his bed. Completely out of breath, I reached for the phone and called my auntie to see if she'd heard from him. Just then, Rich shouted for me to come downstairs. Immediately, I saw was a police officer standing by the front door.

"What's going on, Rich?"

"Baby, sit down."

"No, tell me what's wrong."

"You're dad…he's gone baby. He's dead."

I don't remember what happened after that because I fainted.

~~~

I awoke in my bed, hoping it was all a dream. But when I saw Rich and my auntie Sherry I knew it was real. Rich sat on the bed and hugged me while my auntie handed me a cup of water.

"But, it doesn't make sense." I sobbed into the cup.

"It was an accident. He was drunk. His car crashed and went over a cliff," Auntie explained.

"I don't understand it, either," Rich agreed with me. "I mean, he was doing so good with his sobriety. Something had to upset him to make him turn back to liquor."

As Rich massaged my back, I buried my face in his chest and wept. It was my fault. I had caused it all. But I couldn't say a thing about it. The only thing I could do was hurt like hell.

I got through the funeral and the next week due to Rich, Auntie and April. I forgot about our misunderstanding, and April stayed by my side even more than Rich did. She was the only one I could tell exactly what happened between my dad and me.

"So you think your dad got high again because of you?"

"Yeah," I sniffled.

We had the house to ourselves. Auntie had gone back home and taken Bree with her and Rich had returned to work, so it was just April and me, sitting on my bed together.

"Oh, honey, this is not your fault," April tried to reassure me.

"It is," I said over her words. "Daddy hadn't drunk a thing in years. And then he caught me and Kwame having sex. He got so upset…I've never seen him that mad. I caused this! And I'll never forgive myself. It's my fault he's in the grave. How am I gonna make it without my daddy?"

I burst into tears again, crying so hard I couldn't breathe. April hugged me until I calmed down. We talked for another good hour before I sent her on her way. It was good to be alone. I was tired. All I needed was my pill so I could sleep. Half an hour later the pill started to kick in. Just as my eyes got heavy, I heard the sound of footsteps.

"Rich?"

Because of the pills, the best I could manage was a whisper. No one answered, yet the footsteps kept getting closer. I tried to speak again, only this time my mouth wouldn't cooperate. My eyes clamped shut but I forced them open again. Then the door swung inward. I fought to keep my eyes from closing, but they were too heavy. The last thing I saw was Kwame, standing over me.

Through my medicated fog I felt Kwame run his hand over my hair.

"Oh, Kendra...my sweet Kendra," I heard him croon softly.

My heart raced faster than a speeding car. Then I felt Kwame's lips on my forehead.

"You're so beautiful...so beautiful," he kept saying over and over. I never wanted to do this. But I had no choice."

"Do what?"

It was so hard to speak, and the words came out all slurry. I wanted to ask Kwame why he was in my house. But I couldn't force those words out.

"I love you. I will always love you, Kendra," was the last thing I heard Kwame say.

I stretched my eyes again, but the medicine took over. My eyes shut tight and I was out.

~~~~

I woke up the same way I fell asleep: with my heart pounding. Kwame was at the foot of my bed.

"How'd you get in here?" I shot straight upright.

"I have the keys," he replied.

"How'd you get a key to my house?"

"I live here."

"What? Kwame, you don't live here."

"Kendra, baby, what's wrong?! Are you okay?"

I had to blink a few more times before my head and my eyes cleared and I realized the voice and face belonged to my husband, Rich.

"Oh, shit."

I burned with embarrassment so bad I felt like I had slid down a razor and landed in a river of alcohol. Rich sat on the bed and grabbed my hand.

"Baby, you okay?" he asked again.

"Yeah," I said, temporarily puzzled.

"Good, because I've been worried about you all day."

"I'm fine," I assured Rich. I moved my hand away.

Rich looked at me strangely.

"Why you called me the yardman?"

"I called you the yardman?!"

"You thought I was Kwame."

"He was supposed to come cut the grass today. I guess I was dreaming," I lied smoothly.

Rich stared at me some more, then he rubbed my arm.

"Baby, I know you're still hurt about your dad, but you have to relax and take it easy. You need to put something on your stomach, too. I brought dinner. Let me fix you a plate."

Rich left the bedroom.

That dream I had about Kwame being in my room was so weird it made me shiver. I raked my fingers through my hair and wondered if I was losing my mind. I was about to get out of bed and go to the bathroom when I saw my necklace—the one I'd given Kwame when we he took me sailing. It was on my pillow. My heart began pounding, and pain pulsed through my head.

I hadn't been dreaming. Kwame had been in my house—in my bedroom!

~~~~

My cell phone started to ring the moment Rich walked back into the room with a plate full of food. He reached for my phone and I jumped up to try to get it first. I snatched the phone right before Rich reached it.

"It's probably April," I forced a smile. "Would you mind fixing me something to drink?"

Rich hit his head with his hand.

"I'll be back. I left the drinks in the car."

When I was sure Rich was gone, I viewed my phone display. Sure enough, it was Kwame. That fool never stopped calling me or easing his stupid truck past my house. I didn't want to see him. That would only remind me of Daddy and of what I'd caused. And knowing Kwame had been in my house freaked me the hell out.

He'd left two messages.

Message one:

"Kendra, we need to talk. Call me back now!

Message two:

"Kendra, listen very carefully to me. I need to see you…talk to you…it's important, love. Just call me, okay?"

My nose was flaring while I dialed Kwame's number. He picked up on the first ring.

"Kwame what in the fuck is wrong with you? Why in the hell were you in my house?!"

"I had to see you. I have to talk to you."

"How did you get in here?"

"That's not important—" he began, but I cut him off.

"What…are you sick? Are you out of your mind? You were in my home without my consent. I don't like that. I don't want to talk to you ever again. And don't you ever fucking come in my house no more. Just leave me alone."

"Do you want your husband to find out about us?"

My breath caught in my throat. I did not want to believe what I'd just heard.

"So, you making threats?"

Before he could reply, I heard the front door open. I snapped the cell phone shut and hauled ass to the bathroom. I closed the door and tried to think. Kwame had just threatened me. He was beginning to act like a nut.

"What in the hell have I got myself into?" I said out loud, lowering my face to my hands.

Who knew what Kwame might do. He could sneak in the house and be standing over me and Rich while we slept. I was going to protect myself and my family, just in case. I walked into the bathroom closet and opened the box where Rich kept the household's gun. It was gone.

This shit was getting realer by the second.

17

The man was officially stalking me.

I became paranoid. Kwame was in my neighborhood all the time now. Not only would I see his truck ride by my house, I even saw him following me one day; but when he realized I'd caught him, he turned off at the next corner. And don't get me started on the calls. I just kept my cell phone off. I would only turn it on when I had to make a call away from home. And then I would see his missed calls, messages and texts.

I had the locks on the house changed. Rich questioned why he needed new keys. I told him some bullshit story about how I had lost my purse with my keys and all my information, and he fell for it. I didn't know how many more lies I could tell before Rich caught on to me.

A week later I was at my daycare handling business when April popped by.

"Girl what's going on?"

"Stress."

I put down the paperwork I was going over and wiped the sweat from my forehead. Then I told her all the shit that had happened.

"You think he stole your gun?"

"Who else would take it?"

"This is terrible," April looked just as worried as I was. "You think he's going to tell Rich?"

"Girl, I hope not. I'm all messed up in the head. At first Kwame was nice and sweet; now he just seems off. The day he came in my house he kept saying he had something to tell me, that he wanted to talk. He kept saying he had no choice. I don't know what the hell is going on anymore."

"What are you going to do about it?"

"I might drop by and talk to him after I finish up here. I want to see what he got to tell me."

"Going to see that man will only add fuel to the fire."

"Well, what am I supposed to do? You know I can't tell Rich. Girl, I'm ashamed of myself. I'm so full of regret at what I've done. Do you know how bad I'd feel if he found out? Shit, Rich was trying to look out for me and Bree, and

I was cheating. I can't tell him no funky mess like this. I just hope and pray Kwame didn't mean that shit about telling Rich. I have to stop him from breaking up my family."

I never understood what Daddy meant about listening with your ears and not your heart until now. Kwame had wined and dined me. He said all the right things. But this man is a nut. I should have been faithful to Rich.

April gave me a light hug, and I was unable to hold back the tears.

"Hey, you weren't the first and you won't be the last woman to have an affair. So dry them tears. Don't beat yourself up about it; learn from it. You know what you did was wrong so I am not going to criticize you for it. All I can do is support you."

"Support me?" I asked.

"Yeah?!" she replied like I had said something stupid.

April dried my eyes. I got myself somewhat together.

"We'll, you can start by grabbing some of those papers and helping a sister out."

April laughed. "And what are you going to do to pay me for this hard labor?"

"How about I cook you dinner at my place tonight."

18

Rich

I was home chilling with my homeboy Cory
and playing the new video game he brought
over. It was Cory's turn on the stick, so my mind
drifted to Kendra. Over the last few weeks she
had calmed down a lot, and I was glad we were
getting our relationship together. I was still upset
that Daddy Isaac was gone. But I made up my
mind I was gonna step in and be everything to
Kendra since her pops had departed. That's what
Daddy Isaac would have wanted.

"Dang, this level is hard to pass," Cory
banged on his controller.

"I figured out how to pass it last night."

"We'll, help a brother out," Cory laughed.

The doorbell sounded just as I was ready to show him.

"Hold up," I said, jumping from the couch.

"Bring me a soda and some chips."

"Do I look like your mama? Get off your ass and get it yourself."

When I opened the door, a delivery man was outside.

"I have a delivery for Rich."

"That's me," I said.

He held out an electronic clipboard. I signed it, took the box from him and headed back into the living room.

"What's that?" Cory asked, putting down the game controller.

"Don't know," I replied.

I sat back on the couch and struggled to open it. I was kind of excited 'cause I never got anything. Once I got it opened, I removed a note and some tissue paper. Then I reached inside and pulled out a pair of red silk panties. Immediately I recognized them.

"What the hell?" I said out loud.

Kendra had brought those months ago. When I saw them in her underwear drawer they still had the tag on them. At one point I had begged her to wear them for me, but we weren't getting along at that time because I was working so much. Now, holding, looking and smelling the scent of stale perfume on them, I knew they'd been worn. But for who? Sure wasn't me. I opened and read the note.

The pussy is mines.

~~~~

I read the note over and over again until my eyes turned chili pepper red. I tried to figure out what was going down. Cory took the note from me. After a second he lowered his face.

"Damn, man, this foul. Who sent this?"

I looked at the box but there was no address.

"How they deliver a package without no return address on it? Where they do that at?"

"I don't know, man. They ain't even have your last name. But look at the way Dude was dressed. You know he probably some bullshit local courier."

My brain was going in a million directions. Why would someone mail me my wife's underwear? I grabbed the letter from Cory and looked for any clues.

Cory shook his head.

"Man, I'ma jet. I don't want nothing to do with this."

"What you mean you don't want nothing to do with this?!" I asked.

Cory had a weird look on his face and a strange vibe was coming from him. He had been my boy forever and I knew him better than I knew myself.

"If you know something, tell me. You my boy. We like brothers, man."

Cory slid his hand over his face.

"Man, Kendra fucking around on you," he finally came clean.

"What?!"

I tossed the box aside and stood up, angry that Cory would say something like that about my wife and the mother of my child. Cory began to stutter. He always stuttered when he was nervous.

"I didn't want to tell you but I saw Kendra with that man who does your yard." Cory told me.

"What you mean, you saw her?" I asked, seeing stars.

"They was at Passion's Restaurant a while back, all hugged up and dancing. The next day I came here to confront her ass. I thought I could stop shit before anything happened, but when I got here the door was unlocked and—"

My chest hurt so bad I thought I was having a heart attack.

"And, what, man? Spit it out."

"I saw the two of them in the kitchen."

"What you mean, you saw them in the kitchen?"

"They were fucking."

"You lying bastard."

"I'm not lying," Cory yelled. "Why would I lie about some foul mess like that?!"

I didn't even realize I had Cory jacked up against the wall until I heard Kendra and April's voices shouting and asking me what was going on.

I flipped out. I lost any rationality I had. I picked up the underwear and threw it at Kendra before I jumped over the couch separating us and went for her ass.

19

Kendra

When I saw the rage in Rich's eyes I tried to haul ass, but the next thing I knew, I was on the floor and Rich was on top of me like white on rice.

"You ho!" He banged my head on the hardwood floor. "You fucked the yardman. After all I did...sacrificed for your ass. How could you do some shit like that?"

I tried to tell Rich to get off of me but my brain was scrambled and I was paralyzed with fear. It took April and Cory to pry Rich's hands from around my neck. Once they finally freed me, I didn't try to talk to him. I ran upstairs and closed and locked the door. Then, I cried my eyes out. I didn't know what to do. How had he found out?

Downstairs there was a lot of commotion—mainly shouting. Less than ten minutes later, there was a knock on the door. I didn't answer. I was too scared…ashamed.

"Kendra, it's me." April said. "Rich is gone. He's staying with Cory tonight."

I unlocked the door and dropped to the edge of the bed. I couldn't stop crying or shaking.

"What just happened?" I asked, out of my mind with distress.

"Kwame sent him your underwear in the mail."

I pounded the bed with my fist. How could I have been so stupid? Why did I even mess with a man who would do some sick shit like steal my underwear and mail them to my husband? I went downstairs and found the package and the note. I ripped the letter apart. That sick son of a bitch had fulfilled his threat.

Now my marriage was over.

~~~

The next morning I called Kwame only to find his number had been changed. Later that day a private number started calling me nonstop. I could tell it was Kwame by the heavy breathing on the other end. I got dressed and went to his apartment.

I pounded and pounded on the door until I thought splinters were in my hand.

"Open up, you bastard!" I shouted.

A across the hall door opened instead.

"Ma'am, who are you looking for?" an old woman asked.

"Kwame."

"He moved out."

"Moved out? When?"

"A few days ago."

"Where did he move?"

"I don't know. Now do you mind leaving?"

My blood was boiling. I raced down the stairs to my car. Kwame was gone. It was over. He had broken up my marriage and now he'd vanished. But why in the hell was he still calling me?

~~~~

I called Rich, too, but he didn't want to talk to me. My aunt said she would keep Bree as long as I needed, so I spent the next few days trying to get my head straight. The calls from the private number didn't stop: Kwame called me over one hundred times. He was crazy as hell and I decided to change my cell phone number.

April invited me over to her house the next night. Since I was alone and hurting, I thought it would be a great reprieve. When I pulled into April's driveway I couldn't lie: I was jealous all over again. My friend had it going on. April lived in a big mansion in the toney part of town. Her and her fine husband greeted me at the door.

"Nice to meet you," the man who introduced himself as Andrew said. "I've heard some great things about you.

"Nice to meet you, too," I replied, taking in his handsome features.

April hugged me. "Come in. Let me show you around before dinner."

By the time she'd showed me her entire home I felt like I usually did after I watched an episode of MTV cribs. I felt like I hadn't accomplished shit with my life. April had the fine ass husband. The mansion. And her husband obviously was crazy about her. While we ate our lamb, Andrew held her hand and kissed her. I looked at my plate while tears mixed with my lamb sauce. I should have been working on my relationship with my husband. Instead, I had been working on another man's dick. And what did I have to show for it? A crazy ass stalker on my hands.

April and I had drinks on the balcony after dinner while Andrew departed to do some after-hours work with an overseas client.

"So how are you holding up?" April questioned me.

"My life is a mess. I don't have my man or my daddy. And Kwame is driving me crazy. Has he done your yard lately?"

"No, he changed his number. Anyway, if he had come by, I would have fired him. Has he been in contact with you?"

"I changed my cell number, too, because that nut kept calling me from a private number."

"Do you think you and Rich will get back together?"

"I hope so. The well is dry and I miss it. I called him and asked him to come over tonight so we can talk, but he won't pick up and speak to me."

"Do you want to stay here tonight? I have more than enough room."

I didn't think twice about it. There was no way in hell I'd be a third wheel and watch April and her loving husband while I slept alone.

"No, I'm good. Thank you for the incredible lamb and drinks, but I gotta head home."

I could tell April didn't want me to leave.

"Why don't you have another glass of wine?" she asked.

"No, thanks. Just give me the bottle to take home."

April and I laughed as she walked me to the door.

20

When I got home later that night, I was depressed. I fixed me a glass of wine and checked my home and cell phone messages. Nothing from Rich, just bill collectors. The last message stopped me in my tracks.

"Kendra, this is Kwame. Pick up the phone. Would you please just pick up the phone?"

I cursed several times. Now the psycho was calling my home number. I thought about calling the police, but I didn't want anyone to know I had cheated on my husband and now had a nut stalking me. We lived in a small town and gossip spread too easily. That sort of scandal would hurt Rich and I couldn't do it. I looked out the windows. The street was empty. I made sure all of my doors were locked.

Wine bottle in hand, I was about to go upstairs and get my behind in the shower when I saw a nasty ass worm crawling on the floor. My skin began to crawl. Rich wasn't around to ask and my daddy just wasn't around anymore, period, so I got a paper towel, picked the slimy thing up and flushed it down the toilet. Still shuddering, I jumped in the shower. When I got out, I got my wine glass and went back into my bedroom. This time I saw a spider—a disgusting black spider crawling on the floor.

"What in the hell is going on?" I wondered.

Not only was I mad, now I was feeling icky.

"Tomorrow I'm calling an exterminator," I promised myself. Daddy always had one come out yearly because we lived near the woods and insects and bugs and other horrible creepy crawlers were always on our property.

I watched the spider twirl away in the toilet water then washed my hands. Gulping down the rest of my wine, I strolled into my bedroom and turned out the lights. I was about to pull back the covers when I noticed something moving underneath them. My heart almost leaped through my chest. I pulled back the cover slowly, only to discover snakes, spiders, worms and ants covering my sheet. They were all tangled together, crawling and flipping over each other. One black snake dropped off the bed right near my feet. Screaming, I backed out of the room, ran downstairs and struggled with the lock on the door. When I got it opened at last, I ran right into someone's chest.

~~~~

"Kendra, what's wrong?"

It was Rich. I couldn't stop screaming and crying long enough to tell him what I'd seen upstairs. Finally the words came out. Rich made me stay outside, and a few minutes later he came outside with the sheet tied in a knot. I watched him go toward the woods then reappear a few moments later.

"Who did that, Kendra?"

All I could do was cry. I remembered telling Kwame a while back how much I hated snakes and stuff. I looked up at Rich and muttered the man's name.

~~~~

That night Rich checked me in to a motel. He called a company that would come the following morning to take care of the house. Things were awkward between Rich and I, but Rich stayed with me. As he sat on the hotel bed I told him everything, even how I thought Kwame stole our gun.

"So not only did you cheat on me and fuck this man in our home, but now he's stalking you. Damn it!" Rich dropped his head to his hands. "I'm calling the cops."

"No," I begged. "This is a small town. I don't want anyone to know about this."

"Oh, so now you shamed? You didn't have no shame when this man was fucking you all over my house. You hurt me, Kendra. You disrespected me."

Rich began crying like a baby. I felt lower than whale's shit all over again.

I sat next to him and hugged his back.

"Why did you do this? I had chances to cheat, but I was faithful to you. I loved the hell out of you."

"Rich, I'm sorry. I hurt you because I'm stupid and self-centered."

"I want to leave you," Rich shot up from the bed. "I fucking hate you right now. I swear I do."

It was my turn to cry.

"I don't want you to leave me, Rich. I want my family."

"How can I trust you again?"

"I'll have to prove myself. Show you by my actions and not my words that you can trust me."

"I'll never trust you again, Kendra. Once a cheater, always a cheater."

21

The next few days were like being in Hades. Rich didn't trust me no further than he could throw me. He made me go get checked for STDs. He did the same. Thank God everything came back clean. Then Rich began accusing me of wanting every man we came in contact with. He hated to go to work. Sometimes he would pop up at home or my daycare unexpectedly to see if I was where I'd told him I would be. He knew every place I went and checked to make sure I was there. Rich also had access to my cell phone. We fought every day. I was so stressed my hair began to come out in clumps. The thing that hurt the worst was: Rich didn't want Bree to come home.

"Why can't my baby come home?" I asked.

Kwame hadn't done anything in days and I was beginning to think it was over.

"Bree's not coming back until we move."

"We're moving?"

"Yeah, to Florida. I've already transferred my job and got us an apartment down there."

"What about my daycare…this house?"

"Sell the daycare and the house. We have to start over."

Tears came from my eyes. I saw tears in Rich's eyes, too.

"I can't have my child here and this fool has access to my home. He may have our gun. No one is hurting my daughter or you."

What a fool I'd been to cheat on Rich. He was all man. Rich represented what a man was supposed to be. I came to the conclusion that real love wasn't the dates and the flowers. It was about commitment. It was about the person who would remain during the bad times as well as the good. It was about the person who would always have your back no matter what.

"You're right," I agreed. "We have to move."

I was still sad, though. I would have to move from the only home I'd ever known. So many memories were here. I had grown up in this home and done so many fun things with Daddy here. I wanted Bree to grow up here, too. But I had caused this entire mess and now I had to look out for my child. I had to lay in the bed I had made.

~~~~

A week later, Rich and I had dinner with April and her husband Andrew.

"I'm glad you two are back together," April smiled.

She and I were on the patio. Rich and Andrew were in the house talking men stuff.

"I hate that you have to move to Florida."

"I know. This is my last week here."

April wiped a tear from her eye.

"What am I supposed to do without you?! We've been besties forever."

"We will always be in each other's lives," I hugged her. "You helped me through some rough patches."

April and I were both weeping.

"Once I get settled, I'll invite you and Andrew over."

"You'd better," April smiled. "I would love to feel the Florida sun."

April and I held each other tightly. She promised she would come over to help me pack the next day.

On the way home, Rich and I stopped by my auntie's house and saw Bree. Bree was extremely agitated. After all, our house was the place she had always known as home, and she hadn't been there is several days.

"I'll be back to get you tomorrow. You can help April pack," I swore.

On the way back to the house, Rich grabbed my hand.

"I want to apologize to you." Rich said, giving my hand a squeeze.

"Why?" I asked.

"Because I had no right putting my hands on you the day I found out about you and Kwame. But I…I flipped. When I found out you'd been with another man I just…lost it. I swear I will never do anything like that to you again."

"Please, Rich…don't. I was wrong. I caused everything. I'm so sorry. I will spend the rest of my life showing you how sorry I am."

I wiped away the wetness on my cheeks. I should never have depended on Rich or any other man to make me happy. My happiness was dependent on me. At least now things were slowly falling into place. Rich and I were stronger as a couple and moving forward. I could breathe a little easier. I leaned back against the headrest and looked out into the traffic. Instantly my heart stopped.

I saw Kwame's truck in the side-view mirror. It was right behind us.

~~~~

Rich pulled onto the side of the road.

"I'm sick of this punk disrespecting me," he shouted.

"What are you gonna do?" I yelled back. "You're not gonna do anything stupid, are you?"

I didn't have to wait too long to find out. When Kwame's truck went by, Rich pulled out behind him. He pressed his foot on the gas like he was possessed by a demon and rammed our car into Kwame's rear bumper.

"Rich!" I screamed. .

Kwame pulled over to the side of the road and Rich pulled in behind him. Rich jumped from the car and before I knew it, he was jacking Kwame up.

I leaped from the passenger side door, shouting for Rich to stop.

"I have to see Kendra! I want to talk to her…please," Kwame begged through swollen lips.

He tried to push past Rich to get to me.

"Kendra, I need to tell you something...please hear me out!" he cried.

Rich balled up his fist and punched the shit out of Kwame. Kwame hit him back. They begin to tussle, and the next thing I knew, they were rolling on the ground. The fight continued for minutes with Rich beating Kwame to a pump. The only thing I could do was watch.

A car pulled over. Two men jumped out and somehow managed to break the fight up.

"You stay the fuck away from my family or I'll kill you!" Rich shouted as the stranger pushed him back towards our car. "I promise, I'll kill your ass!"

Once he was back in the car I looked over Rich's bloody face. I was unable to stop crying. The little bit of pleasure I experience with Kwame was not worth the trouble I was going through.

I had invited the Devil into my home and now I was experiencing Hell.

22

That night when Rich was asleep, I got on the phone and called the only person I could talk to: April.

"I don't get it, April. I'm lost. What in the hell does Kwame want to tell me? Shit, maybe I need to just talk to him."

"Are you just as crazy as he is?" April snapped at me.

"No, but maybe if I talk to him he'll tell me what he has to tell me and move on."

"The man is a psycho. Rich will never go for that."

"I'm not planning on telling Rich."

"What are you planning on then?"

"I'm going to find out what's going on. I'm telling you, something about this entire situation is off. I'm gonna find Kwame and get to the bottom of it."

"Do you think that's wise? Rich is already having trust issues. If he finds out about this, it will really send him over the edge. Think about your marriage. When you go to Florida this will all be behind you."

I sniffed loudly and wiped the moisture from my red, burning eyes.

"Look, I started all of this. Now I'm about to lose everything. I can't let Kwame run us away from our home…our town...our life. I have to fix it."

"I don't agree with this plan. But I'm here for you. What can I do to help?"

"I just need for you to help me finish packing tomorrow. I also need you to keep Bree while I look into this."

~~~~

"I'm way more comfortable leaving you, knowing April is here," Rich told me the next morning when he left for work. Since this was our last day in town, Auntie had also dropped off Bree.

"Girl, please hurry up and do whatever it is you're gonna do," April begged. "I wouldn't want Rich to come back and find you gone. I'd be in a sticky—not to mention awkward—situation."

"I'm hoping Rich won't call me all day 'cause he knows you and Bree are here with me. If Rich does call or come back, just tell him I went to U-Haul to rent our truck. Then call me right away."

April grabbed my hand. "Please, be careful."

"I will," I promised.

I gave Bree a kiss on the forehead. I was doing this for her…for my family.

I went back to Kwame's apartment complex, walked into the management office and asked for the rental manager.

"Yes, how can I help you today?"

It was some old bleached-blonde woman with green eyes. I swallowed all my fears and put on my game face.

"Can I speak with you in private?"

"Sure, if you don't mind waiting until I handle the rest of my tenants."

Ten minutes passed. I listened as the manager talked with renters. She bragged about her kids and talked about how hard it was to be a single parent. Meanwhile, I practiced what I would say to her in my head over and over. There was no time for fear. Daddy always told me that when you had a child you couldn't be afraid of anything because that child trusted in you to protect and take care of it. How weird. Here was another of Daddy's sayings that didn't make sense until he was dead and gone. I had to develop crocodile skin with the quickness. All I could do now was hope that the apartment manager would fall for my story.

Finally, the office was empty. I took a seat at the desk.

"Please, just call me Kendra," I told the apartment manager who'd identified herself as Ms. Evans.

"Kendra," Ms. Evans let out a deep breath and leaned back in her office seat. "I cannot give you Kwame's personal information. As a landlord, I cannot and do not give out personal information unless the police have a warrant or summons."

"But it's very important," I didn't let up.

Ms. Evan's hard scowl became even rougher looking.

Plan A isn't working. Time for Plan B, I thought. I looked at the pictures of Ms. Evan's children displayed proudly on her desk. I remembered some of the things she'd said in the office earlier to her tenants about how hard it was being a single parent. I pulled out my Kleenex.

"You don't understand. I'm in trouble."

Ms. Evans flashed a frown.

"You see. Kwame and I were dating and now I'm pregnant," I lied.

I let big fat fake tears run down my cheeks and off my chin: crocodile tears to match my crocodile skin.

"I already have three children and I just lost my job because of health issues. I don't know what I'll do if I have to do this on my own again. I really need to find out where he moved."

Ms. Evans held up her hand. Her face lightened a bit. Her eyes fell on the picture of her three children before she lifted them back up to me.

"Listen, I would really like to help you. Believe me, I know how hard it is. I'm a single parent myself. But I just can't."

I was about give up and to get ready to leave when Ms. Evan's rose from her desk.

"Wait right here. I'll be back in few seconds," she told me.

Removing a folder from her file cabinet, Ms. Evan's withdrew a sheet of paper and made a copy of it. Once she was done she balled the copy up and told me to follow her. Confused as hell, I did. Before we made it to the door, Ms. Evan's dropped the balled up paper in the empty trash can.

"I'm going to have to excuse myself. Do you mind throwing away the trash for me?"

"Not at all," I grinned. "Thank you," I mouthed on my way out.

She didn't know how much she had just helped me.

~~~~

Inside my car I stared at the crumpled paper. Kwame's new address seemed very familiar. I was sure I had been on that very street before. I called April and told her I would be home soon.

"Give my baby girl a kiss, will you?"

"Just hurry back," April begged me. "I'm worried sick about you and I don't want Rich to come here and find you gone."

"Well, stop worrying. I'll check in later."

I put on my sunglasses and pressed the gas.

23

The closer I got to Kwame's new address the more confused I became. I stopped at the address and looked at the beautiful mansion. This had to be a mistake. Why had he put April's address down as his new place of residence?

I parked in the driveway. Pulling out my cell phone, I dialed April to tell her I'd run into a dead end. I also wanted to tell her that Kwame was using her address. But as I flipped the phone open the door to April's home opened also. An elderly White female stepped outside with a flowerpot in her hand. As she walked in my direction I took off my sunglasses and stepped outside the vehicle.

"Is there something I can help you with?" she asked.

"No ma'am," I smiled to set her at ease. "My friend and her husband live here. She didn't tell me she had visitors."

The old White woman looked baffled.

"I'm sorry. You must have the wrong address. This is the Pursers' residence. My husband and I have lived here for over twenty years."

"I'm sure this is my friend's home, ma'am. I've been here twice. My husband and I ate dinner here just last week."

"There must be some mix up. What is your friend's name?"

"April."

"April Thomas?" The old woman placed the pot on the driveway. "I'm afraid you are mistaken. April does not live here. She is my house sitter. April lives at 511 Edgefield."

A dizzy spell hit me out of nowhere. Nothing was making sense. I was about to ask another question when a car pulled into the driveway.

"I can clear this up right now, Mrs. Purser. That's April's husband, Andrew."

"His name is not Andrew," Mrs. Purser said. "That's Jeff. He is my yardman."

When Andrew noticed me, he put the car in reverse and backed out, screeching off down the road. I stumbled back to my car, heart beating so hard it made my eyes throb. Trying to catch up with Andrew, who I now knew was Jeff, I backed out of the driveway so fast I knocked down Mrs. Purser's recycle bin. I had to find out what the hell was going on. April had lied. Why had she lied? Why had Jeff, or Andrew, or whatever the hell his name was, also lied? And why was he doing over one hundred miles per hour trying to get away from me? Something was wrong—terribly wrong. The light ahead turned red and I knew I was about to catch up with him, but Jeff/Andrew ran the red light and drove right in front of a Mack truck.

"Oh, my God!" I screamed as I watched his mangled car being dragged down the street.

~~~~

My heart was racing out of control as I drove away from the scene. I had to put this puzzle together. According to Mrs. Purser, 511 Edgefield was April's real address. That was less than ten minutes away. I sped off, finding April's home with little trouble. The place was a real hellhole. With its caved-in front porch and junky yard, the dilapidated house could have been abandoned, and should have been condemned. The area was heavy with prostitution and drug activity. I looked at the mailbox and sure enough: April's last name was on it. Next, I knocked on the front door. When no one answered I peeped in a side window, but dark curtains prohibited my view. I went around the back and wiggled the knob. Locked.

"Shit!"

I noticed the top of the door was glass. I picked up a rock and knocked out the window pane, stuck my hand in and unlocked the door.

Cautiously, I stepped inside. A foul odor made me gag. In the messy kitchen right away I saw mail and also some schoolwork from Creekside Elementary—more signs that April really lived there. And then I saw something that made my heart stop—

A picture of April and Kwame hugging.

They knew each other on a personal level.

I had been set up!

A shiny object on the table caught my attention.

It was Daddy's ring. His class ring. The one he never took off.

I vomited on the floor.

"Oh, God! No!" I cried as I backed out of the house and hauled ass to my car.

My hands were shaking so bad I couldn't get the keys in to start the car. My cell phone began ringing. It was Rich.

"Baby, where are you?" he asked me.

"On my way home. Man, do we have to talk."

"I'm at home now. April said you went to get more boxes."

"Rich listen to me," my voice was shaking. "I want you to get Bree and get the hell out of that house."

"What are you talking about?"

"Please, baby, just trust me. I found out some foul shit about April. She—she's a liar, Rich. I believe she killed Daddy. And she's involved in this situation with Kwame. Andrew isn't even her husband. Everything she told us is a lie!"

The phone went dead.

"Rich! Rich!" I screamed into the line. I burned rubber all the way home.

24

Rich

I was on my stomach on the kitchen floor, groaning in pain and wondering what in the hell had just happened. I'd been on the phone with Kendra when I felt a sharp pain in the back of my head. I blacked out for a moment. Now I was awake and wondering why was blood dripping from my head onto the floor. Why did my head feel so achy and woozy?

I turned over onto my back. April was standing over me with demonic eyes. Her face was twisted so much that she looked like a monster.

"April... what are you doing with that gun?" I asked.

Then it dawned on me: she had just snuck up behind my ass and hit me upside the head with it.

"Kendra knows, doesn't see?" April shouted, ignoring my question. "That bitch knows everything."

"What are you talking about?" I asked, scooting backwards away from her. My mind was on my wife and child. I wanted them to be safe.

"That was Kendra on the phone, wasn't it?"

"No," I lied.

"Lie to me again and I'll blow your head off your fucking shoulders!"

April aimed the gun at me.

I held up my hands. "Okay, okay. Yes…it was Kendra. What's going on? You're Kendra's best friend. Why are you doing this?!"

"You and your whore of a wife will find out soon enough. Get your ass on the couch and don't you dare move."

I did as I was told and stumbled to the couch.

"Where is my daughter?"

"Upstairs."

"Is she okay?"

April smiled a wicked smile that resembled the Joker's.

"She's safe for now. But her future safety depends on you and that bitch you call your wife."

25

Kendra

My heart stopped when I saw Rich's car still in the driveway. I ran into my house, not bothering to shut the door.

"Oh my God, Rich!" I shouted when I saw his head bruised and bleeding.

The door shut and April appeared with a gun pointed at me.

"I must say I'm shocked it took you this long to find out."

"You killed my father."

"Yep, the bastard came home early and caught me in here going through your personal things. I couldn't risk him telling you and ruining my plan. So I took him for a ride in his

Cadillac and forced him to drink a whole bottle of liquor, then, when he was good and drunk, I sent his car over a cliff."

My eyes filled up with water.

"You set everything up with me and Kwame, too, didn't you?"

"Yes, bitch," April smiled like she was enjoying everything. "I also paid Jeff to pretend he was my husband. I had to make myself look good. Like I was the married, caring friend who had your back."

"Jeff's dead," I said, hoping it would get a reaction out of her.

"I know. I was on the phone with him when he got into that accident. He's the one who told me our cover was blown."

The water ran freely down my face.

"Why... Why did you do this, April? You're my best friend."

April snorted.

"When will bitches learn? A woman can never be another woman's real friend. Bitches always have an underlying motive for hanging around another female. I learned that from you in high school."

"What are you talking about? I never betrayed you. I was a true friend to you."

"You didn't fuck my boyfriend, Tony?"

"That was years ago. We were teenagers. I didn't do it to hurt you. It didn't mean anything to me."

"Didn't mean anything? I loved him! He was the first man who loved me for me. Tony looked passed my skin disease and my lazy eye. He was going to marry me, until you began flirting with him and took him away."

April waved the gun.

"You were always so fucking selfish, Kendra. You were the spoiled, pretty bitch who always got everything—even my man. And then you moved on with your life and got married to Rich—a man who worshipped you like a god— but you still weren't satisfied. So I made a plan.

"You see, I couldn't let you go on after you took my man and my chance at happiness away. Oh, no. I made it my mission to come back here and destroy your life and your marriage. I knew you would fall for Kwame the moment I laid eyes on him. He was just your type and the perfect person I could use. Kwame came to the U.S. illegally. I hired him to work for me, and I promised I'd help him get a green card if he did me a favor."

"What sort of favor?" I asked, tasting bitter bile in my mouth.

"The plan was: Kwame would seduce you, collect evidence and then break up your marriage," April waved the gun again as she spoke. "But the fucker ended up falling in love with you. Can you believe that shit? I don't know what the hell you got between your legs but it must be better than platinum because it made him turn on me. He backed out and told me he was gonna tell you everything. So I had to kill the bastard."

~~~~

"You killed Kwame?" I gasped.

"Yeah, he should be maggot food right about now with all of this summer heat."

Sobs shook my body.

"Of course, when the cops find Kwame they're gonna think Rich did that shit."

"What are you talking about?" Rich demanded.

"I shot his ass with your gun."

Rich and I both gulped.

"Since you fought him last night in public, and people witnessed you saying you were gonna kill him, the cops will have an open and shut case."

"What are you planning to do with me and Kendra?" Rich asked.

"Now we on the good part," April sneered. "Get your asses up! Move it!"

26

April shoved me into the bedroom right behind Rich. My clothes were all over the floor,
although some of them were inside a suitcase on
the bed. On top of the clothes in the suitcase was
another gun—our gun that April had stolen and
killed Kwame with. Bree was sitting next to the
suitcase, lost in her own little world.

"Bree!" I shouted, ready to run and hug her.
But April stopped me.

"Get your ass against the wall," she ordered.

"April, please," Rich begged. "Let my wife and daughter go. Hurt me. Not them."

"Oh, how sweet. You want to play Captain Save A Ho? Sorry, Rich. She has to pay. This bitch greatly deserves everything she's about to get."

"What are you gonna do to me…to my family?" I whimpered.

"It's simple. I'm going to have Rich shoot you and then turn the gun on himself. When the cops find you two, it will look like Rich murdered Kwame, came home and found you packing to be with your lover, and killed you before turning the gun on himself."

"The detectives will figure out foul play was involved," I tried to discourage her.

"Never," April insisted.

She flipped on the television. Images of me and Kwame having sex on the boat flashed on the screen.

"You sick cunt," I cried. "You had him steal my underwear and record us together."

April laughed. "Yeah and I have every note, email and text you sent him. How does it feel to see your wife fucking another man's brains out?" she asked Rich.

Rich turned and dropped his head. I wanted to tell him I was sorry I had ruined his life. My dad always told me that sometimes pain was the only thing that could change some people's evil ways.

How true.

"What about my child?" I asked. "How do I know you won't kill her after you kill us?"

April snickered. "I'm heartless, but that little bitch has nothing to do with this. As long as you do what I say, she'll live. However, she will remain in this house with you and Rich's dead body until someone finds you two."

"I'm not shooting my wife!" Rich shouted.

"Oh, yes you will shoot this ho," April walked over to Bree. "Or I'll shoot your daughter right in the head. I really don't give a fuck. Try me and see."

"No!" I cried. "Please don't hurt her."

"Then let's get busy. I don't have all day."

~~~~

I couldn't comprehend any of this. I was about to die and my husband would have to do it. April was gonna get away with the perfect crime all because of me and my selfish stupid ways. She forced me to stand in front of the bed. Then she made Rich get our household gun. Finally, April moved behind Bree with her firearm.

"Please don't hurt my baby!" I cried.

Rich was crying too.

"I can't…I can't kill you, Kendra."

"You have to shoot me or she'll kill Bree," I screeched at him.

April put the gun to my baby girl's head.

"Can you shoot this bitch, please?!" she said impatiently. "It shouldn't be hard. The woman fucked a man she hardly knew in your home. She told me she wanted to divorce you."

Rich looked at me with the most pained expression I'd ever seen on his face. His eyes were wide and a large vein was throbbing in the middle of his forehead. I had to make Rich focus. Otherwise, there would be three dead bodies instead of two, and there was no way I would let my daughter die over something I had done.

"Do it, Rich," I yelled. "Shoot me. April is right: I was planning to leave you. I don't love you," I lied. "Just shoot me, damn it!"

Rich looked out of his mind. He lowered the gun and succumbed to his tears.

"I'm warning you," April shouted. She cocked the gun. "On the count of three, I will pull the fucking trigger on your daughter if you don't! One…"

Slob was coming from Rich's mouth, he was crying so hard.

"Two…"

"Kendra, I love you," Rich whispered.

"Three."

I felt fire hit me in the stomach. It knocked me down on the bed. I struggled to breathe. The room began to fade away into darkness. I looked at Rich one final time, then at my daughter. It was hard to think this would be my last time seeing them. If I had to do it all over again, I would have listened to my daddy. I never would have cheated and I never would have told a woman all of my business. But it was too late. I felt life draining from my body along with my blood. I told the world goodnight.

27

Rich

"Kendra!" I yelled.

I dropped to my knees. I couldn't stop crying. The love of my life was gone. It was so over-whelming I felt like I would die from my own grief. I was ready to give up. And then Bree started to cry. Her eyes were on her mother. Bree rarely made eye contact with me or her mom. But at this moment she knew her mom was gone. I would be next. What sort of life would my child have? And what if April didn't keep her word? What if she killed my daughter? There was no way in hell I would let that happen.

"Get your ass up!" April ordered me, crazy assed smirk on her face.

I did as she instructed, then I began to laugh.

April's face caved in.

"What the fuck is so funny?"

"You are. You're pathetic. You'll never get away with this."

"Sure I will. I created the perfect plan."

"Did you really?"

"Who the fuck you think you playing mind games with?" April's grin got wider. "On my dumbest day, I'd be one hundred steps ahead of you."

"Really? Then why don't you know about the cameras I installed last week?"

"There are no cameras in this house," April shouted.

"Sure there are. Kendra doesn't even know about them," I lied. "I had them installed right after she found those snakes in our bed. Everything you're doing is being recorded, dummy."

"Liar!" April's hands began to shake.

She moved away from Bree and brandished the gun at me instead. Suddenly, Bree jumped up and flew under the bed. April dropped to her knees and aimed toward where Bree had fled. Before April could fire, I shot the gun in my hand at her. She stood and popped off two shots back at me. I ran from the room. A second later I felt agonizing pain in my arm. I managed to make it down the stairs and into the living room, dodging bullets the whole way. Unable to hold on, the gun dropped from my hand onto the floor. That's when my legs gave out. I didn't know April had shot me in the leg, too, until I saw the blood. She flew into the living room right behind me. I couldn't stand up so, in an effort to get away, I used my feet to slide across the floor. April took her time closing the gap between us. When she reached me at last, she kicked me in my side.

"Where the fuck are the cameras?" she pointed the gun at my dome.

"I'll show you." I held up my hands. "Just let me get up."

Using the chair for support I pulled myself up, hobbling into the kitchen.

"Move your ass!" She hurried me along.

"Wait, my leg is hurting."

"Your ass will be hurting if you don't move it now!"

Turning quickly, I grabbed the open container of bleach on the counter and dashed it in April's face. Her hands shot up to protect her eyes. Her gun slid under the refrigerator. I grabbed her and we began to scuffle all over the kitchen floor.

The woman fought like a man, landing blows all over my face and upper body. Somehow I gained the upper hand on her. Using my good arm, I put her in a choke hold. April struggled for a few seconds before I felt her body go limp. Then I felt a searing pain in my private area. Helpless, I curled up in a ball.

"Fucker!" April hocked and spat on me. Breathing hard, she made her way to her feet. I could hear Bree crying from the bedroom.

April staggered over to the refrigerator and fished her gun out from under it. She wiped blood from her mouth and then tasted it. She laughed.

"I'm going to kill you, then your daughter," she announced.

She aimed the gun and proceeded to pull the trigger.

"NOOOOO!"

I shot up and rammed my body into April's full force. She landed on the opened dishwasher door. I retrieved April's gun from where it had fallen, just inches from her outstretched hand. I turned, ready to fire every bullet in the gun at her. April wasn't moving, though.

Kendra's dad had always told Kendra about leaving the dishwasher open and the knives turned sharp side up. Daddy Isaac said Kendra was going to kill somebody one day. It appeared his prediction had come true. A knife was sticking up through April's chest. Blood was oozing from her mouth. She was dying and there wasn't a thing she could do but await Hell's flames.

I wanted to finish April off, but at the same time I didn't want death to come too soon for her. I wanted her to suffer. Then I heard Bree crying again. I stuck the gun in my pocket and lurched out of the kitchen. I wanted to search for the gun I had dropped earlier in the living room, but Bree needed me.

Upstairs, Bree was not under the bed; she was lying on her mother's chest. Sobbing, I went to pull Bree off of her mom. She didn't need to see Kendra dead. But when I looked down I noticed Kendra's eyes were open. She was alive, barely, but she was still holding on. I kissed her.

"Hang on, baby. I'm calling an ambulance now."

~~~~

The sound of laughter behind me stopped me dead in my tracks. A bloody April was reeling toward me with a gun.

The gun I had dropped earlier in the living room.

28

Kendra

The bitch just wouldn't die, I thought as I watched her aim the gun at Rich. She had destroyed my life, yet like a cat with nine lives, she just kept coming back. I knew I had to do something. I saw the gun in Rich's side pocket. He might not have time to get it and shoot her but I sure as hell did. With the little strength I had left, I pulled the gun out of his pocket and shot April over and over until the gun was empty.

April fell to the floor. Now that I knew my husband was okay, I could die in peace. With no energy left, the gun slipped from my hands. Rich kissed me gently.

"I… I'm sorry," I fought with my last bit of strength to tell him. "I didn't mean any of those things I said earlier. I do love you. Take care of… take care of Bree."

Darkness washed over me.

Epilogue

Kendra

"SHE'S GOING INTO SHOCK!" a woman dressed in all white shouts.

She and another man lift me from a stretcher and place me on what feels like a hard table.

Shock? What the hell is that? All I know is I'm tired. More tired than I've ever been in my life. I can't take in even one lungful of air and I don't feel anything. My eyes feel like they're turning into hard marbles.

Another man dressed in all white hovers over me.

"LET'S GET HER TO THE OPERATING ROOM NOW!" he shouts.

~~~~

I want to ask him what's going on. Why is he shouting in my ear? And where is my daughter, Bree? Worried out of my mind I try to sit up, but it feels like a sumo wrestler is on my chest. Everything starts moving in slow motion, then the world slowly begins to fade away. About ten people push my bed down a long corridor.

It feels like I'm being sucked down a drain. Lifting my head a little, I look at the wet red shirt I'm wearing. My memory comes rushing back. The shirt isn't red–my upper body is covered with blood from the gunshot wound my husband inflicted on me.

~~~~

I remember everything that happened.

On the count of three I am lifted off my gurney and placed on a table, where the ridiculous tubing is removed and a mask is placed over my face. I pray the Lord will let me make it through this.

If He does, I promise I will be a changed woman.

Rich

I toss the red rose on the casket and close my eyes. It's been a week since my entire life was turned upside down. I sit on the foldout chair and watch the workers throw dirt over the coffin.

"Rest in peace," I whisper.

Long after the funeral is done I'm still perched on that foldout, wondering how I can pick up the pieces and go on with my life. I've been through so much. Still, I gotta be strong. I gotta move on. I gotta somehow take what's left and make a life out of it.

I got a daughter to look after.

My cell phone starts ringing.

"How was the funeral?" the voice on the other end asks.

I smile.

"I made sure he was put away nicely," I reply.

"I can't believe you paid for Kwame's funeral," Kendra says.

She's still in the hospital recovering from her bullet wound. Although Kendra has a long way

to go, the doctors say she should heal completely.

"Paying for Kwame's funeral was the least I
could do," I mutter. "The man was trying to
warn you about April. Even though what he did
was wrong, he must have realized that, because
he was trying to protect you," I have to admit.

I finally raise up off that hard-assed seat and
stare at the fresh dirt Kwame is buried under. I
allow myself to cry for a little while, thankful
my family had survived. I'm thankful we have a
second chance.

"I love you so much," I tell Kendra.

"I love you, too," she says back.

I can tell Kendra is sobbing. She hasn't been
able to sleep a full night since the accident and
neither have I or Bree. I'm happy we'll be moving to Florida once Kendra is released. I hope the
move will help us heal our family and move
forward.

"Do you think we'll ever be able to get past
this?" Kendra asks.

I dry my eyes.

"We will," I promise. "It's not gonna be easy.
But we will get through this, with God's help."

Dear Reader

Dear Readers,

Thank you for reading, Infatuated.

Please visit our website:

www.ahsyadpublication.com

Facebook: Ahsyad Publication Bookreaders

God bless and thanks again for the support!